SHADOWS IN FLIGHT

By Orson Scott Card from Tom Doherty Associates

Empire
The Folk of the Fringe
Future on Fire (editor)
Future on Ice (editor)
Hidden Empire
Invasive Procedures (with
    Aaron Johnston)
Keeper of Dreams
Lovelock (with Kathryn Kidd)
*Maps in a Mirror: The Short Fiction of
    Orson Scott Card*
*Pastwatch: The Redemption of
    Christopher Columbus*
Saints
Songmaster
Treason
The Worthing Saga
Wyrms

ENDER

Ender's Game
Ender's Shadow
Shadow of the Hegemon
Shadow Puppets
Shadow of the Giant
Speaker for the Dead
Xenocide
Children of the Mind
First Meetings
Ender in Exile

HOMECOMING

The Memory of Earth
The Call of Earth
The Ships of Earth
Earthfall
Earthborn

THE TALES OF ALVIN MAKER

Seventh Son
Red Prophet
Prentice Alvin
Alvin Journeyman
Heartfire
The Crystal City

WOMEN OF GENESIS

Sarah
Rebekah
Rachel & Leah

From Other Publishers

Enchantment
Homebody
Lost Boys
Magic Street
Stonefather

Stone Tables
Treasure Box
*How to Write Science Fiction
    and Fantasy*
Characters and Viewpoint

SHADOWS IN
FLIGHT

Orson Scott Card

TOR®

A TOM DOHERTY ASSOCIATES BOOK
NEW YORK

SHADOWS IN FLIGHT

Copyright © 2011 by Orson Scott Card

A Tor Book
Published by Tom Doherty Associates, LLC
175 Fifth Avenue
New York, NY 10010

www.tor-forge.com

Tor® is a registered trademark of Tom Doherty Associates, LLC.

Library of Congress Cataloging-in-Publication Data

Card, Orson Scott.
    Shadows in flight / Orson Scott Card.—1st ed.
        p. cm.
    "A Tom Doherty Associates book."
    ISBN 978-0-7653-3200-4
    I. Title.
    PS3553.A655S535 2012
    813'.54—dc23
                                            2011042468

First Edition: January 2012

Printed in the United States of America

0 9 8 7 6 5 4 3 2 1

For Lynn Hendee
wise guide, fellow maker, true friend

SHADOWS IN FLIGHT

CHAPTER 1

In the Giant's Shadow

The starship *Herodotus* left Earth in 2210 with four passengers. It accelerated nearly to lightspeed as quickly as it could, and then stayed at that speed, letting relativity do its work.

On *Herodotus*, just over five years had passed; it had been 421 years on Earth.

On *Herodotus*, the three thirteen-month-old babies had turned into six-year-olds, and the Giant had outlived his life expectancy by two years.

On Earth, starships had been launched to found ninety-three colonies, beginning with the worlds once colonized by the Formics and spreading to other habitable planets as soon as they were found.

On *Herodotus*, the six-year-old children were small for

their age, but brilliant beyond their years, as the Giant had been when he was little, for in all four of them, Anton's Key had been turned, a genetic defect and a genetic enhancement at the same time. Their intelligence was beyond the level of savants in every subject matter, without any of the debilitations of autism. But their bodies never stopped growing. They were small now, but by age twenty-two, they would be the size of the Giant, and the Giant would be long dead. For he *was* dying, and when he died, the children would be alone.

In the ansible room of *Herodotus*, Andrew "Ender" Delphiki sat perched on three books atop a seat designed for adults. This was how the children operated the main computer that processed communication through the ansible, the instant communicator that kept *Herodotus* linked to all the computer networks of the ninety-four worlds of Starways Congress.

Ender was reviewing a research report on genetic therapy that showed some promise, when Carlotta came into the ansible room. "Sergeant wants a sibmoot."

"*You* found me," said Ender. "So can he."

Carlotta looked over his shoulder at the holodisplay. "Why do you bother?" she said. "There's no cure. Nobody's even looking for it anymore."

"The cure is for us all to die," said Ender. "Then Anton syndrome disappears from the human species."

"We'll die eventually," said Carlotta. "The Giant is dying now."

"You know that's all Sergeant wants to talk about."

"Well, we have to talk about it, don't we?"

"Not really. It'll happen, and then we'll deal with it." Ender did not want to think about the Giant's death. It was overdue, but as long as the Giant lived, Ender could hope to save him. Or at least bring him good news before he died.

"We can't talk in front of the Giant," said Carlotta.

"He's not here in the ansible room," said Ender.

"You know he can hear us here if he wants."

The more time Carlotta spent with Sergeant, the more she sounded like him. Paranoid. The Giant is listening.

"If he's hearing us now, he knows we're having a meeting, and what it's about, and so he'll listen wherever we are."

"Sergeant feels better about it when we take precautions."

"I feel better when I'm allowed to do my work."

"Nobody in the universe has Anton syndrome except us," Carlotta said, "so the researchers have all stopped working on it even though there's perpetual funding. Get over it."

"They've stopped and I haven't," said Ender.

"How can you research it without lab equipment, without test subjects, without anything?"

"I have this incredibly brilliant mind," said Ender cheerfully. "I look at all the genetic research they're doing and I'm connecting it with what we already know about Anton's Key from back in the days when top scientists were working hard on the problem. I connect things that the humans could never see."

"We're humans," said Carlotta wearily.

"Our children won't be, if I can help it," said Ender.

"'Our children' is a concept that will never have a real-world example," said Carlotta. "I'm not mating with either of my male sibs, which includes you. Period. Ever. It makes me want to puke."

"The idea of sex is what makes you puke," said Ender. "But I'm not talking about 'our children' in the sense of any of us reproducing together. I'm talking about the children we'll have when we rejoin the human race. Not the normal children, like our long-dead sibs who stayed with Mother and mated and had human children of their own. I'm talking about the children with turned Keys, the children who are little and smart like us. If I can find a way to cure *them*—"

"The cure is to discard all the children like us, and keep the normal ones, and poof, Anton syndrome is gone." Carlotta always came back to the same argument.

"That's not a cure, that's extinction of our new species."

"We're not a species if we can still interbreed with humans."

"We're a species as soon as we find a way to pass along our brilliant minds without the fatal giantism."

"The Giant's supposedly as brilliant as we are. Let him work on Anton's Key. Now come along so Sergeant doesn't get mad."

"We can't let Sergeant boss us around just because he gets so angry when we don't obey."

"Oh, brave talk," said Carlotta. "You're always the first to give in."

"Not at this moment."

"If Sergeant walked in here himself, you'd apologize and drop everything and come. You're only delaying because you're not afraid to annoy me."

"Just as you're not afraid to annoy *me*."

"Come on."

"Where? I'll join you later."

"If I say it, the Giant will listen in."

"The Giant will track us anyway. If Sergeant is right and the Giant spies on us all the time, then there's nowhere to hide anyway."

"Sergeant thinks there is."

"And Sergeant's always right."

"Sergeant *might* be right and we can humor him and it costs us nothing."

"I hate crawling through the air ducts," said Ender. "You two love it, and that's fine, but I hate it."

"Sergeant is being so *nice* today that he picked a place we can get to without going through ducts."

"Where?"

"If I tell you, I have to kill you," said Carlotta.

"Every minute you take me away from my genetic research you're bringing us that much closer to death."

"You already made your point, and it's an excellent point, and I'm ignoring you because you *are* coming to our meeting if I have to drag you there in small pieces."

"If you regard me as expendable, have the meeting without me."

"Will you abide by whatever Sergeant and I decide?"

"If by 'abide by' you mean 'ignore completely,' then yes. That's what your plans deserve."

"We haven't made plans yet."

"Today. You haven't made plans yet *today*."

"Our other plans all failed because you didn't follow them."

"I followed every plan I agreed with."

"We outvoted you, Ender."

"That's why I never agreed to majority rule."

"Who's in charge, then?"

"Nobody. The Giant."

"He can't leave the cargo bay. He's not in charge of anything."

"Then why are you and Sergeant so afraid he might be listening in?"

"Because all he cares about is us, and he has nothing to do but spy on us."

"He does research, just like me," said Ender.

"That's what I'm afraid of. Results: zero. Time wasted: all of it."

"You won't feel that way when I come up with the invasovirus that carries the cure to our giantism into every cell of your body and allows you to reach a normal human height and stop growing."

"With my luck, you'll switch off Anton's Key and make us all stupid."

"Normal humans aren't stupid. They're just normal."

"And they forgot us," said Carlotta bitterly. "If they saw us again, they'd think we were nothing but children."

"We *are* children."

"Children our age are just learning to read and write and do their numbers," said Carlotta. "We are more than a quarter of the way through our expected life span. We're the equivalent of twenty-five years old, in their species."

Ender hated it when she threw his own arguments back at him. He was the one who argued that they were a new species, the next stage in human evolution, *Homo antoninis,* or perhaps *Homo leguminensis,* after the Giant, who had used the name "Bean" for most of his childhood. "They won't see us again, so they won't treat us like children," said Ender. "I'm not content with a life span of twenty years, nor with death by overgrowing the capacity of our own hearts. I don't intend to die gasping for breath while my brain dies because my heart can't get enough blood to it. I have *work* to do and an absolute deadline for doing it."

Carlotta apparently was tired of bandying words. She leaned in close and whispered. "The Giant is dying. We have things to decide. If you don't want to be included in the decisions, *ever,* then by all means skip this meeting."

Ender hated thinking about the Giant's death. It would mean that Ender had failed, that whatever he learned later would have come too late.

And something else, too. A deeper feeling than frustration at failing to reach a goal. Ender had read about human feelings, and the words he thought came closest were "anguish" and "grief." He could not speak of this, however, because he knew what Sergeant would say. "Why, Ender, I believe you're saying that you *love* the old monster." And love, they knew, was a thing that came from the human side, from Mother, and Mother had chosen to stay behind on Earth so her ordinary human children could lead ordinary human lives.

If love meant anything, the children had long ago concluded, it would have kept Mother with them, and their ordinary siblings, all of them on this ship, all of them looking together for a cure, for a new world, for a life together as a family.

When they were not yet two years of age, they said this to Father. He was so angry he forbade them to criticize their mother again. "It was the right choice," he said. "You have no understanding of love."

That was when they stopped calling him Father. As Sergeant said, "It was their decision to break the family. If we have no mother, then we have no father, either." He was "the Giant" from then on. And they did not speak of Mother at all.

But Ender thought of her. Did she feel, when we left, what I feel now, thinking of the Giant's dying? Anguish? Grief? They decided what they thought was best for their children. What would the life of the normal siblings be on this ship, if they had kept the family together? They would be larger than Sergeant, Carlotta, and Ender, but they would feel like great stupid oafs, never able to keep up with the antonines, the leguminotes, whatever they decided to call themselves. Mother and the Giant were right to divide the family. They were right about everything. But Ender could never say that to Sergeant.

You could never say anything to Sergeant that he didn't want to hear.

It was a recapitulation of human history, right here on the *Herodotus,* that the most angry, aggressive, and violent of the three children was the one who always got his way. If we're a new species, we're only somewhat improved. All the alpha-male nonsense of the chimps and gorillas is still preserved in us.

Carlotta turned her back on him and started out of the room.

"Wait," said Ender. "Can't you tell me what this is really about? Why are *you* always in on it, and I get things sprung on me with the two of you already in agreement, and no time for me to research anything or even come up with a decent argument?"

To her credit, Carlotta looked a little embarrassed. "Sergeant does what he wants."

"But he always has you for an ally," said Ender.

"He could have you, too, if you didn't always resist him."

"He doesn't give me a chance to resist, he doesn't listen. I'm the other male, don't you see? He has you under his control and me off balance because he intends to be the alpha."

Carlotta frowned. "Mating is still a long way off."

"It's already being determined by our choices now. Do you think Sergeant will take no for an answer?"

"We won't let him have his way on that."

"We?" said Ender. "What's this *we*? There's you and him, and then there's me. Do you think you and I will suddenly become *we* just because *you* don't want to have his incestuous babies? If we're not *we* now, not ever, then why do you think I'll risk my own survival to save you then?"

Carlotta blushed. "I will not talk about this."

But you'll think about it, Ender said silently. I made you think about it, and you won't let go of it. The alliances we make now will be the alliances then. He'll be the alpha male, you'll be the devoted mate, and I'll be the nonmating subjugated male, powerless to do anything but what the alpha commands. If he hasn't killed me first. That's the choice you're making now.

"Let's go hear what Sergeant has to say," said Ender. "Not that you don't already know."

"I really don't," said Carlotta. "He doesn't let me in on what he's thinking any more than he does you."

Ender didn't bother arguing with her, but it simply wasn't true. Or if she really didn't know, then she was always quick to come up with arguments to justify whatever nonsense Sergeant was trying to put forward. She always *sounded* as if she had agreed with Sergeant's program even before he presented it.

We're still primates, only a few genes away from the hairless chimps that began to cook their food so that women stayed by the fire to do the cooking while their monogamous mates ranged and hunted to bring home meat. And only a few genes farther from the hairy chimps that mated whenever they could, usually by force, and lived in terror of displeasing the alpha male.

The main difference is we come up with justifications and explanations, and we manipulate each other with words instead of violent displays or affectionate grooming. Or rather, our violent displays and affectionate grooming *are* words, so they take less energy, but do the same job.

"I'll pretend to believe you," said Ender aloud, "in order to pretend that I think my presence at Sergeant's meeting will do anything but prove his dominance over our pathetic little tribe."

"We're a family," said Carlotta.

"Our species hasn't existed long enough to evolve the family yet," said Ender. But it was mere grumbling. He followed her into the bridge, where she pushed the manual lever to open the trap down to the maintenance shafts surrounding the plasma conductors, the ramscoop collector, and the gravity lens.

"Yes, let's spend hours here, and the whole question of founding a species becomes moot," said Ender.

"The shielding works, we're not scooping much anyway, and shut up," said Carlotta.

They went on down to engineering, which was Carlotta's bailiwick. While Ender persisted with the genetic research that was the whole reason for this voyage, Carlotta had become the onboard expert on mechanics, plasmatics, gravity lensing, and everything else to do with the workings of the ship. "It's our world," she often said, "we might as well know how it works." And more recently she had bragged, "If I had to, I could build the whole thing from scratch."

"From parts, you mean," Sergeant had said.

"From ore in the mountains of some undiscovered planet," said Carlotta. "From the metals in two asteroids and a comet. From the wreckage of this ship after a collision with a meteor." Sergeant had laughed, but Ender believed her.

Carlotta led the way back to the lower lab.

"We could have walked down the corridor to the upper lab and skipped the whole trap door business," Ender pointed out.

"The Giant can hear our footsteps from the upper lab."

"Do you think he can't hear everything, everywhere?"

"I know he can't," said Carlotta. "There are dead spots all over the ship where he can't hear anything."

"That you know about."

Carlotta didn't bother to answer. They both knew that Ender didn't actually care whether the Giant heard them or not—it was Sergeant who had to conceal everything, or at least believe that he was concealing himself.

Aft of the lower lab was the elevator shaft that led back to life support. During strong acceleration phases, the back of the ship became the bottom of a deep well, and the elevator made it possible to go down to life support at the base—and back up again. But in flight, gravity was polarized the other direction, so that the elevator became a simple walkway, at ten percent of Earth normal, leading aft to life support.

The payload area of the ship, where the Giant lived because he couldn't fit anywhere else, was directly above them.
So they walked slowly and lightly, being careful to make no
noise. If Sergeant heard them, he'd be furious because it meant
the Giant could hear them, too.

Sergeant wasn't in life support, though he had the fans running full blast to pump freshly oxygenated air through the
ducts and muffle sound. Ender could never decide whether it
smelled like fresh air or decay—the lichens and algae that
lived in hundreds of large trays under fake sunlight were constantly dying, their protoplasm then getting incorporated into
the next generation in a continuous cycle.

"You know what this place needs?" said Carlotta. "A dead
fish. To improve the smell."

"You don't know what a dead fish smells like," said Ender.
"We've never seen a fish."

"I've seen pictures, and all the books say fish smell bad
when they rot."

"Worse than rotting algae," said Ender.

"You don't know that," said Carlotta.

"If rotting algae smelled worse, then the saying would be,
'Algae and visitors begin to stink after three days.' "

"None of us knows what we're talking about," said Carlotta.

"And yet we keep talking," said Ender.

Ender expected to find Sergeant in the Puppy—the maintenance craft that was programmed by the Giant to remain
within five meters of the surface of *Herodotus* no matter

what contrary instructions it might be given. Ender knew Carlotta had tried for months to untether the Puppy, but she couldn't defeat the programming.

Things like that made it clear to Ender, if to neither of the others, that the Giant was every bit as smart as they were, and he had years of experience behind him. All of Sergeant's precautions were pointless, because at his oversized console in the payload area, the Giant could do whatever he wanted, hear and see and probably smell whatever he wanted, and his children could do nothing about it, nor even detect his spying.

The others refused to believe it, but Ender understood that they were children. Anton's Key meant their brains were still growing—and so was the Giant's brain. His capacity was so far beyond theirs by now that it was a joke to think of out-smarting him. But such was Sergeant's competitive nature that he not only believed he *could* outsmart the Giant, he believed he already had.

Delusional. One of your children is insane, O Giant, and it isn't me and it isn't the girl. What are you going to do about it?

All right, not insane. Just . . . warlike. While Carlotta studied the engineering of the ship and Ender studied the human genome and methods of altering it, Sergeant studied weapons, wars, and means of death. He came by it naturally—the Giant had been a great military commander on Earth, perhaps the best that ever lived, though if he was, Mother had not been far behind him. Bean and Petra—the most powerful weapons in the Hegemon's arsenal as he united the world under a single government. It was only to be expected that some of their children would be warriors at heart, and that was Sergeant.

Even Carlotta was more warlike than Ender. Ender hated violence, hated confrontation. He just wanted to do his work and be left alone. He could see one of his sibs do something remarkable and he had no urge to match or surpass them—on the contrary, he was proud of them, or frightened for them, depending on whether he approved of whatever stunt they were attempting.

Carlotta removed a narrow panel from near the ceiling of the access shaft.

"Oh, not really," said Ender.

"We fit just fine," said Carlotta. "You're not claustrophobic, are you?"

"It's the gravity lensing field," said Ender. "And it's active."

"It's just gravity. Ten percent of Earth. And we're sand-wiched between two plates, it's not like we can fall."

"I hate the way it feels." They had played in that space when they were two-year-olds. It was like spinning around until you were dizzy. Only worse.

"Get over it," said Carlotta. "We've tested it, and sound re-ally does get nullified in here."

"Right," said Ender. "How are we going to hear each other speak?"

"Tin can telephones," said Carlotta.

Of course they weren't the toy sound transmitters that they had made when they were really little. Carlotta had long since reengineered them so that, without any power source, they transmitted sound cleanly along ten meters of fine wire, even around corners or pinched in doors.

Sure enough, there was Sergeant, his eyes closed, "meditating"—which Ender interpreted to mean that Sergeant was plotting how he would take over all the human worlds before he died of giantism at age twenty.

"Nice of you to come," said Sergeant. Ender couldn't hear him, but he could read his lips and besides, he already knew it was exactly what Sergeant was likely to say.

Soon they were hooked up in a three-way connection with Carlotta's tin cans. They all had to lie in a line with their heads turned, Ender between Carlotta and Sergeant so he couldn't decide to end the conversation and slither out.

As soon as Ender crept into the gravity field, he had felt that sense of plunging over the top of a waterfall or leaping off a bridge. Down down down, said his sense of balance. Falling! warned his limbic node, all in a panic. For the first few minutes in the gravity field, Ender couldn't stop himself from flailing about in the startle reflex every ten seconds or so, but that's why Carlotta taped his tin can to his face, so he couldn't knock it away in one of his paroxysms.

"Get on with it," said Ender grimly. "I've got work to do and this place feels like continuous death."

"It's thrilling," said Sergeant. "Humans spend money to get

inside a gravity field for the adrenaline rush, and here we get this one for free."

Ender said nothing. The more he demanded that they hurry, the more Sergeant would digress and delay.

"For once I agree with Ender," said Carlotta. "I programmed turbulence into the lens and it's getting to me."

So Ender was right that it felt worse than usual. For only the ten-thousandth time in his life, Ender wished he had beaten the kuso out of Sergeant when they first met. It would have established a different pecking order.

Instead, Ender had paid attention when Mother kept telling him about how the other kids were "just as much our genuine children as you," even though Ender had actually been born from Mother's body and the other kids had been implanted in the wombs of surrogates.

For the normal kids, that was no big deal—they would have no memories of living anywhere else. But the antonines, Sergeant and Carlotta, were aware of everything at six months instead of three years. They remembered their surrogate families and felt like strangers with Mother and Father.

Ender could have bullied and bossed them, but he didn't. He tried not to imply that he thought of himself as the "real" child, though at the age of twelve months, of course he felt that way. Sergeant's reaction to the strange situation was to assert himself and try to take control. He must have been hell for his surrogate parents in the first year of his life. They would have had no idea what to do with a child who talked in full sentences by six months, who climbed everywhere and got into everything by nine months, who was teaching himself to read at age one.

Carlotta, on the other hand, was reticent; her surrogate parents might not have known just how much she could do at such an early age. When Father and Mother brought her home, she responded to the new situation with shyness, and she and Ender quickly became friends. Sergeant, feeling threatened, had to turn everything into a contest—or a fight.

Ender mostly evaded Sergeant's belligerency. Unfortunately, Sergeant took that to mean submission. Except when he took it as arrogance. "You don't compete because you think you've already won everything."

Ender didn't think he'd won. He just thought of competition with Sergeant as a distraction. A waste of time. It's not fun playing with somebody who absolutely *has* to win, every single time.

"The Giant is taking a long time to die," said Sergeant.

In that instant, Ender understood the entire meeting. Sergeant was getting impatient. He was son of the king and ready to inherit. How many times had *this* script been acted out in human history?

"So what do you propose?" asked Ender neutrally. "Evacuate the air from the payload area? Poison his water or his food? Or will you insist we all hold knives and stab him to death?"

"Don't be melodramatic," said Sergeant. "The bigger he gets, the harder it will be to deal with the carcass."

"Open the cargo bay and jettison it into space," said Carlotta.

"No," said Sergeant. "More than half our nutrients are tied up in his body and it's beginning to affect life support. We have to be able to reclaim those nutrients so we have something to eat and breathe as *we* get larger."

"So we cut him up into steaks?" asked Ender.

"I knew you'd react that way," said Sergeant mildly. "We won't eat him, not directly, we'll slice him and put him in the trays. The bacteria will dissolve him and the lichen will have a growth spurt."

"And then double rations for everybody," said Ender.

"All I propose is that we stop feeding him his full daily calories. By the time he notices, he'll have become so feeble that he can't do anything about it."

"He won't want to," said Ender. "As soon as he realizes we're trying to kill him, he'll want to die."

"Melodrama!" said Sergeant. "Nobody wants to die, unless they're insane. The Giant wants to live. And he isn't sentimental like you, Ender. He'll kill us before he'll let us kill him."

"Don't assume that the Giant is as evil as you," said Ender.

Carlotta tugged on his foot. "Play nice, Ender," she said.

Ender knew how this would play out. Carlotta would express her regret but she'd agree with Sergeant. If Ender tried to give the Giant extra calories, Sergeant would beat him and Carlotta would stand by, or even help hold him. Not that the beatings ever lasted long. Ender just had no interest in fighting, so he didn't defend himself. After a few blows, he always gave in.

But this was different. The Giant was dying anyway. That caused Ender enough anguish that the idea of hastening the process was unbearable.

Nothing unbearable had ever been proposed before. So Ender's reaction surprised even him. No, *especially* him.

Sergeant's head was right there, just above Ender's own. Ender reached up, and with all the power of his arms, he rammed Sergeant's head into the wall.

Sergeant's hands immediately snaked out to begin the battle, but Ender had taken him by surprise—no one had ever actively hurt Sergeant before, and he wasn't used to dealing with pain. By the time Sergeant's hands were groping for Ender's arms, Ender's legs were braced on both sides of the field containment shaft and he was ramming the heel of his hand full strength into Sergeant's nose.

Blood sprayed out and floated in globules that "fell" in every direction in the turbulent gravity field.

Sergeant's grip faltered. This was serious pain. Ender could hear him shouting in fury into the tin can.

Ender shaped his hand into a fist and drove a knuck into Sergeant's eye.

Sergeant screamed.

Carlotta twisted on Ender's foot, shouting, "What are you doing? What's going on?"

Ender braced himself against her grip and drove the edge of his hand into Sergeant's throat.

Sergeant choked and gasped.

Ender did it again.

Sergeant stopped breathing, his eyes bugging out in terror.

Ender pulled himself along until his mouth was over Sergeant's. He locked their lips together and blew into Sergeant's mouth, hard. He got blood and snot from Sergeant's nose inside his mouth when he did, but he couldn't avoid that; he hadn't yet decided whether to kill Sergeant. The rational part of Ender's mind, which had always been in control till now, was beginning to reassert itself.

"Here's how it's going to be," said Ender. "Your reign of terror is over. You proposed murder and you meant it."

"He didn't mean it," said Carlotta.

Ender lashed back with his foot and caught her in the mouth. She cried out and then just cried.

"He meant it and you would have helped him with it," said Ender. "I've put up with this goffno till now but now you crossed the line. Sergeant, you're not in charge of anything. If you try to give orders to anybody again, I'll kill you. Do you understand me?"

"Ender, he'll kill *you* now!" cried Carlotta through her tears. "What's happened to you?"

"Sergeant will not kill me," said Ender. "Because Sergeant knows that I just became his commanding officer. He's been dying to have one, and the Giant wouldn't do it, so I will. Since you don't have a conscience of your own, Sergeant, you will have mine from now on. You don't do anything violent or dangerous without my permission. If you catch yourself thinking about harming me or anyone else, I'll know it because I can read your body like a big-print book."

"No you can't," said Carlotta.

"I can read the human body the way you read the machinery on the ship, Carlotta," said Ender. "I always know what Sergeant's planning, I just never cared enough to stop him until now. When the Giant dies, of his own accord, in his own good time, then we will probably do something like what you proposed, Sergeant, because we can't lose the nutrients. But we don't need those nutrients now and we won't need them for years. Meanwhile, I'll do all I can to keep the Giant alive."

"You would never kill me," croaked Sergeant.

"Patricide is a thousand times worse than fratricide," said Ender, "and I won't even hesitate. You didn't have to cross this line, but you did, and I think you knew what I'd do. I think you wanted me to do it. I think you're terrified by the fact that nobody ever stopped you from doing anything. Well, this is your lucky day. I'm stopping you from now on. You and your weapons and your war games—I learned how to damage the human body and I can promise you, Sergeant, I have permanently changed your voice and your nose. Every time you look in the mirror, every time you hear yourself talk, you'll remember—Ender is in charge and Sergeant will do as Ender tells him. Got it?"

As punctuation, Ender wrung Sergeant's nose, which was definitely broken.

Sergeant cried out, but that hurt his throat terribly and he gurgled and choked and spat.

"The Giant's going to ask what happened to Sergeant," Carlotta said.

"He won't have to ask," said Ender. "I'm going to repeat our conversation to him, verbatim, and the two of you will be there to listen. Now, Carlotta, back down this shaft so I can drag Sergeant's miserable body out to where we can get the bleeding stopped."

CHAPTER 2

Seeing the Future

Bean looked at his three children and it was only with effort that he concealed the depth of his grief and fear for them. He had known it was only a matter of time, and while he was relieved that Ender had finally woken out of his long pacifist slumber to end Sergeant's domination, he knew that they had only set the scene for conflict to come. What will happen when I'm gone? thought Bean.

Petra, I have botched this completely, but I don't know how I could have done it better. They've had too much freedom, but I couldn't chase them through corridors where my body no longer fit.

"Andrew," said Bean, "I appreciate your loyalty to me, and the fact that you repeated all conversations verbatim, including the incredibly stupid and dangerous things you said."

Bean watched as Ender blushed a little—not from embarrassment, but from anger. He also saw how Carlotta looked a little relieved, and Cincinnatus—Bean had always hated the nickname "Sergeant"—got a sudden look of triumphant hope. These children had no idea how transparent they were to him. Learning to read other people took time, no matter how clever a child might be.

Though they might be better at it than Bean supposed. What if they knew exactly what emotions they were showing now, and let them show deliberately?

Petra, you got the easier bargain. I never thought how challenging it would be, raising children who were so grimly determined to survive—however they chose to define that—and so preternaturally good at acquiring the skills to do it.

I must have been just a little terrifying myself at that age, if anyone had cared to notice. If Achilles had understood me only a little better, he would have killed me and not Poke. But Achilles was insane, and killed out of need rather than policy.

Ender had the self-control not to plead his case, despite the criticism, nor to try to build more of a case against the others. Instead he stood patiently, despite that slight blush, which was already fading.

"Bella," said Bean to Carlotta.

"That's not my name," she said sullenly.

"It's the name on your birth certificate."

"On a world I will never see again."

"Carlotta, then," said Bean. "You do understand that avoiding conflict by constantly allying yourself with the stronger brother is not going to work, because these boys are evenly matched."

"No one knew that until today," said Carlotta.

"I did," said Bean.

"I still don't," said Sergeant.

"Then your absurd self-esteem is completely undeserved, Cincinnatus. Because it was very careless of you to think that Ender was only what he seemed. Though if he were truly a killer, you'd be dead now, taken utterly by surprise."

Sergeant flashed a tiny microsmile.

"No, Cincinnatus," said Bean. "The fact that Ender is not a killer does not mean he won't kill you, if he feels the need. You see, you're an attacker, a competitor, and you don't understand what Ender is—a defender, like the boy I named him for. Just because he feels no need to control other people doesn't mean he'll let you take what he doesn't mean for you to have—including my life. Including his own."

"Thank you for the lesson, Father," said Sergeant. "I am always wiser after these little interviews."

Bean let out a roar—a long one, and so loud the whole cargo compartment vibrated. The children visibly quailed before him. Not long ago, they would have knelt. By reflex—Bean had never asked them to do so.

"You stand charged with planning my murder, Cincinnatus. Perhaps a faint effort at showing rue would be better than open snottiness."

"What are you going to do, Father? Kill me? You know I was right. You're an unproductive drain on our—"

"I know that you're still so young and ignorant that you think you don't need me any longer," said Bean. "But someday you *will* reenter the human universe, completely unprepared for what you'll find there because you're so filled with arrogance that it doesn't cross your mind that there are *many* humans who are more than a match for you."

Sergeant said nothing.

"I have lived among them. On the streets of Rotterdam as a child I survived among human beings at their most feral, and found among them human beings at their best and most civilized. I know how humans make war. I know how they plot murder. I know what they care about—a thousand different things that you know nothing of. And to kill me now, when I've taught you almost none of that—"

"Why *haven't* you taught us?" demanded Carlotta. "You haven't even told us enough for us to know that we didn't know enough yet."

"You didn't seem ready or interested," said Bean. "But since my heart might give out at any time, perhaps I should begin your lessons. Let's start with this: People resent it when you try to kill them."

"I'm sorry if I caused you resentment," said Sergeant. His imitation of regret was getting better, but it was still not good.

"They tend to try to kill you back. You're clever, Cincinnatus, but you're also tiny. An ordinary ten-year-old could kill you without much effort. An adult could break you in his hands."

"Could they?" said Sergeant. "My research tells me that there's a strong resistance to killing infants."

"Then your research is inadequate. Alpha males of a certain type kill children by instinct, and it takes all of society's efforts to keep them from doing so at the slightest provocation. You provide provocations that are more than slight."

"We're your children," said Carlotta. "You told us the story of Poke and Achilles, how you told Poke to kill Achilles the first time you brought him into your jeesh."

"We called it a 'family'—the jeesh was something else, later. And yes, I told her to kill Achilles and I was right, because Achilles was a sociopath who had to kill anyone who had humiliated him. I didn't know that until I saw him on the ground, humiliated, and then I knew. He posed a direct threat. For the defense of Poke and the children she protected, he had to die. She didn't kill him, and so he eventually strangled her and threw her in the Rhine. How does that apply to our situation here?"

"You consume so much of our resources," began Sergeant.

"I consume exactly twice as many calories as an ordinary human adult, and the three of you combined consume as many as one adult, which adds up to the consumption of three on a ship that can sustain twenty adults for ten years, or five for forty years. I'm puzzled at your sense of crisis about this, Sergeant. Why do you feel a need for me to die? Have I been too burdensome a taskmaster?"

"I was making a point," said Carlotta, "and as usual you digressed in order to talk to one of the boys."

"I wish your mother hadn't given you that special message about feminism. It's made you prickly about nothing, Carlotta. You brought up my insistence on killing Achilles, and apparently your point *wasn't* that because I wanted to kill a dangerous enemy when I was your age, you should be planning to kill people."

Carlotta looked nonplussed. "I guess that was my point. In a way."

"I answered it. Why weren't you listening? I was in a kill-or-be-killed situation on the streets of Rotterdam. If we didn't kill Achilles, he would kill us, and he ended up doing many terrible things before he died. All you have against me is my consumption—so as long as we're making analogies, I came to Poke's group as a starving toddler."

"Our size," said Carlotta, skeptical.

"Smaller," said Ender. "I read his metrics when he was tested for Battle School and that was after his group had been eating well for months. We were big fat bruisers compared to him at the same age."

"You've been studying his records?" asked Carlotta.

"Suck-up," murmured Sergeant.

"He's the only test case for Anton syndrome prior to us," said Ender. "Of course I've studied every scrap of information on the course of his physical and mental development."

"To continue my response to Carlotta's false comparison," said Bean. "I was one more mouth to feed and I didn't look like I could contribute anything to her small group of children. Poke could have kicked me out—they could have beaten me to death for even trying to join them. Many groups had done such things and worse. I had been watching and I saw that she was merciful, within the limits that the brutal conditions of street life allowed. Unlike me today, I posed a definite threat to their survival—a drain on their resources, unlikely to help them gather more. But she heard me out. Do you understand that? Killing wasn't her first response to a genuine threat. She gave me a chance."

"And her mercy got her killed later," said Sergeant.

"Not her mercy to me," said Bean.

"Yes, it *was* her mercy to you," said Sergeant. "The way you talked her into keeping you was by proposing your plan to get a bigger boy to be your protector so you could get into the soup kitchen for one decent meal a day, right?"

Bean saw where he was going, but he'd let him finish. "Right."

"And you even suggested Achilles as the obvious boy because he was big but he had a limp so he needed Poke's group to help him forage as much as you needed him to protect you from bullies and thieves."

"I was right on every point except the choice of Achilles, and I was only wrong about him for reasons that I couldn't know until I saw his response to our tackling him and physically subduing him."

"But if she had simply had her group drive you away from the start, she wouldn't have died."

Bean sighed. "What was foreseeable, Sergeant? My plan worked perfectly, and everybody in the group ate better. Maybe

Poke would have lived longer without my mistakes, but those kids were all living on the margin, and some of them would certainly have died. I didn't foresee murder—but I got the social dynamics exactly right."

"I think Carlotta's example is exactly right," said Sergeant. "When you're surrounded by enemies, you have to be ruthless."

Time to roar again. "Where are your enemies, you stupid git!"

Sergeant quailed again, but the kid had spunk. "The whole human universe!" he shouted back.

"The whole human universe doesn't know you exist, or care either," said Ender mildly.

"They should know!" Sergeant shouted, whirling on his brother. "They made promises and they didn't keep them! They've abandoned us!"

"They have not," said Bean. "The people who actually made the promises kept them, and so did the next generation, and so did the next."

"But they found *nothing*," said Sergeant.

"They found more than two hundred possibilities that didn't work, though some still show some promise. That's a lot of something, to anyone who knows how science works. Maybe we have to find five hundred dead ends before we reach the right answer, and they helped us enormously."

"But they stopped." Carlotta was just as stubborn as Sergeant.

"That doesn't make them our enemies. After all, Carlotta,

you and Sergeant have done absolutely nothing to help Ender and me in our research. By your reasoning, *you* are our enemies as much as they are, and in your case you're ignoring our own self-interest."

"This ship is our world!" Carlotta answered hotly. "For all we know we'll be living here our entire lives. Somebody needs to know how to repair and rebuild every aspect of it."

"I know how," said Bean.

"But you can't do anything, you live in this box where you hardly dare exert yourself because you'll have a coronary episode and die."

"I can control the Puppy remotely from here, and I've done so several times when repairs were necessary."

"And when you die, who'll do it then? Me," said Carlotta. "I didn't abandon your project to cure Anton syndrome, I worked on a project every bit as important to our survival."

"That's true," said Bean, "and I approve of it. I shouldn't have lumped you in with Sergeant when I turned his accusation back on him."

"And I'm preparing to defend us against our enemies," said Sergeant.

"That's complete kuso," said Bean. "It took you about three days to figure out how to weaponize the ship's equipment, and you spend a few minutes a day working out so you're strong and agile enough to fight—if we happen to have enemies who are really short and don't take you by surprise and only come at you one at a time, like in the vids. The rest of the time you've spent fantasizing about nonexistent enemies, then trying to force your sibs into living in your paranoid universe."

"When we run into enemies, you'll be glad I spent time—"

"All of you are geniuses," Bean said sharply. "When an enemy comes any of you is capable of outsmarting them, without spending week after week living in this absolute *madness.*"

"You're calling me insane," said Sergeant. "This from the great warrior who installed Peter Wiggin as Hegemon." He turned to Ender. "I didn't study the Giant's metrics, I studied his battles."

"I didn't install Peter as anything," said Bean. "I helped him quell the wars that threatened to consume the human race after we beat the Formics."

"Speaking of which," said Sergeant, "you were twice as good a strategist and tactician as that kid you named Ender for."

"But I wasn't half as good a commander because I didn't know how to love or trust anybody until I learned it from your mother, years later. You can't command men in war if you don't know how to trust, and you can't defeat an enemy if you don't know how to love."

"I don't have to command anyone in battle because there's nobody to command. There's just me."

"Nobody to command, and yet you spend your life bossing your brilliant sibs and manipulating them. The opposite of a good commander—a tyrant who's too terrified of imaginary threats to recognize rational advice when he hears it."

"The worst thing Mother ever did was leaving *you* to raise us alone," said Sergeant. "Calling me names."

"How dare I," said Bean. "The son who plotted to murder me, and I dare to call him names. Stupid is how you act, it's a name you've earned. Look at you—supposedly preparing to face all enemies, and your brother just mashed your face and your throat so you look like meat and you sound like a creaking door."

"He sprang on me without warning!" Sergeant shouted.

"Stupid again," said Bean. "You were introducing an entirely new element into your little world—the murder of Ender's father. And you were so hopelessly ignorant of him that it never crossed your mind that he would react differently to this threat than he had to all your previous bullying."

"He wasn't my enemy," said Sergeant.

"He's been the only enemy you faced since you first met him when Petra and I finally located all of you and brought you together when you were one year old. The other male antonine. The rival. You've done nothing that wasn't designed to keep him under your thumb for the past five years. Your imaginary enemies are all surrogates for Andrew Delphiki. You've designed humiliation after humiliation for him, manipulating your sister to side with you against Ender, and here's the sad result. Ender and Carlotta are productive members of our little four-person society, as am I. But you, Cincinnatus Delphiki, are a drain on our resources, producing nothing of value and disrupting the functioning of everyone else. Not to mention criminal conspiracy to commit first-degree murder."

To Bean's surprise, tears filled Sergeant's eyes. "I didn't ask to be on this voyage! I didn't want to go! I didn't like you, I liked Petra, but you never even asked what I wanted!"

"You were only a year old," said Bean.

"What does that mean to an antonine! You weren't even a year old when you escaped from the lab where they were disposing of your fellow experiments! We could talk, we could think, we had feelings, and you didn't even ask, we were just ripped out of our homes and you and Petra announced that you were our *real* parents. This big ugly giant and an Armenian military genius. I wanted to stay with the family that was raising me, the woman I called Mother, the ordinary-sized, hardworking man I called Father, but no, you and your wife *owned* us. Like *slaves*! Taken here, sent there, your *property*. And I end up here? In space, near lightspeed, while the rest of the human race moves through time eighty-five times faster than we do. Each year of our lives is a whole lifetime for members of the human race. And you talk to me about *my* crimes? I'll tell you why I want you dead. You stole me from my real family! You gave me your emossin' Anton's Key and then you took away everybody who ever cared about me and trapped me here with an inert giant and two weaklings who don't even have the sense to know they're slaves!"

Bean had no answer. In the five years of this voyage so far, it had never crossed his mind that the children might remember the women who had borne them when, as embryos, they were stolen and dispersed around the world, implanted in women who had no reason to suspect they were the in vitro offspring of the great generals Julian Delphiki and Petra Arkanian.

"Well damn," said Bean. "Why didn't you say something before?"

"Because he didn't know that this is what was pissing him off until right now," said Ender.

"I knew all along!" Sergeant tried to shout, but now his voice had given out entirely. It was just a rasp in his throat.

"You're not going to get your voice back for a month," commented Carlotta mildly.

"The birth families were all stupid," said Ender, "except mine. The others were terrified of us. Yours was no different. They could hardly bear to touch you, they thought you were a monster, you told us that yourself."

"Well what's *this* family," Sergeant whispered fiercely. "Father is a talking mountain in the cargo hold, and Mother is a hologram who says the same things over and over and over and over and over and over."

"She can't help that," said Carlotta. "She's dead."

"The others got to know her, they lived with her, she talked to them every day," said Sergeant. "We have the Giant."

Bean lay back and stared at the ceiling. Then he closed his eyes because he couldn't see the ceiling anyway. Closing his eyes squeezed out the tears that had filled them.

"It was a terrible choice," said Bean softly. "No matter what we did it would be wrong. We didn't talk to you about it because you didn't have enough experience of life to make an intelligent choice. You three were doomed to die by age twenty or so. We thought we'd find a cure quickly—ten years, twenty—and you could come back to Earth while you were still young enough to have your whole lives ahead of you."

"The genetic problem is very complicated," said Ender.

"If we'd stayed on Earth, you'd all be long since dead. Your normal sibs lived to be what, a hundred and ten?"

"Two of them," said Ender. "All got at least a century."

"And you three would have been a sad little memory—long-ago siblings who had a tragic genetic defect and *died* with only one-fifth of a life."

"One-fifth of a life is better than this," whispered Sergeant.

"No it's not," said Bean. "I've had that one-fifth of a life, and it's not enough."

"You changed the world," said Ender. "You saved the world twice."

"But I'll never live to see you get married and have children," said Bean.

"Don't worry," said Carlotta. "If Ender and you don't find a cure for this, I'm never having children. I'm not passing this thing on to anybody."

"That's my point," said Bean. "When Petra and I conceived you, it was because we believed there was a scientist who could sort things out. He was the one who turned Anton's Key in me in the first place. The one who killed all my fellow experiments. We never meant to do this to you. But it was done, and all we could think to do was whatever it took to give you a real life."

"Your life is real," said Ender. "I'd be content with a life like yours."

"I'm living in a box that I can never leave," said Bean, clenching his fists. He had never meant to say anything like this to them. The humiliation of his own self-pity was unbearable to him, but they had to understand that he was right to do whatever it took to keep them from getting cheated the way he had been. "If you spend the first five or ten years of your life in space like this, so what? As long as it gives you the next ninety years—and children who will have their century, and grandchildren. I'll never see any such thing—but you will."

"No we won't," whispered Sergeant. "There *is* no cure. We're a new species that has a life span of twenty-two years, apparently, as long as we spend our last five years at ten percent gravity."

"So why do you want to kill me?" asked Bean. "Isn't my life short enough for you?"

In answer, Sergeant clung to Bean's sleeve and cried. As he did, Ender and Carlotta held each other's hands and watched. What they were feeling, Bean didn't know. He wasn't even sure what Sergeant was crying for. He didn't understand anybody and he never had. He was no Ender Wiggin.

Bean tracked him now and then, checking in with the computer nets through the ansible, and as far as he could tell, Ender Wiggin wasn't having much of a life, either. Unmarried, childless, flying from world to world, staying nowhere very long, and then getting back to lightspeed so he stayed young while the human race aged.

Just like me. Ender Wiggin and I have made the same choice, to stay aloof from humanity.

Why Ender Wiggin was hiding from life, Bean could not guess. Bean had had his brief sweet marriage with Petra. Bean had these miserable, beautiful, impossible children and Ender Wiggin had nothing.

It's a good life, thought Bean, and I don't want it to end. I'm afraid of what will happen to these children when I'm gone. I can't leave them now and I have no choice. I love them more than I can bear and I can't save them. They're unhappy and I can't fix it. That's why I'm crying.

CHAPTER 3

Watching the Sky

Carlotta was doing gravity calibrations in the field footing at the very back of the ship when Ender came in to life support, which was just above where she was working. Or just forward of it, depending on how you thought of the ship.

Gravity lensing made everything so confusing. The trays of lichen and algae and bacteria, which generated oxygen for the ship and also created the basic stuff used by the food processors, had to remain level, regardless of what the ship was doing. During acceleration there was no need to do anything at all—inertia gave the trays their proper "down" toward the rear of the ship. But during normal flight, the trays would be weightless, which was why the gravity lensing field had to be configured to give the trays an unaltered down, always toward the rear.

Not only that, the lichen required at least half of Earth-normal gravity. But in the cargo hold just forward of—or above—life support, half a gee would kill Father in about an hour. His heart couldn't take it. And since gravity from thousands of stars was being lensed, and the lensing had to be adjusted constantly as they drew nearer to or farther from the most massive stars, constant adjustments had to be made.

Carlotta had charged herself with the duty of making sure the gravity gauges were always in perfect calibration, so the ship's computers were working with accurate data about incoming gravitation and the lensed gravity in various parts of the ship. She had wired the cargo hold with so many failsafes that alarms sounded if there were the slightest variation in the gravity affecting Father. Here in life support, the tolerances were much more robust. But she still had to make sure the lichen had enough gravity that it didn't overgrow vertically and start shading the lower levels of each tray so that the algae could still photosynthesize at the lowest levels of the trays.

Each tray was essentially a six-centimeter rain forest, with the lichens as the jungle trees, their intricate lacework structure rising as high as the gravity would allow, while light filtered down to the slow-flowing river below, where several varieties of algae created minihabitats for hundreds of different bacteria living in constantly shifting symbiosis. All the processed waste from the four humans—most of which came from Father, though the children's output was no longer negligible—was dripped into the trays at a fairly steady rate, and around each drip source the bacteria had the job of de-composing it into nutrient soup that the algae and, eventually, the lichens could live on.

Bacteria also ate decaying lichen and algae and each other. It was a bug-eat-bug world in there, yet a carefully contained one, so that nothing spilled. Then, one by one, the trays were automatically pulled out, skimmed of most of the lichens and some of the algae, then replaced to begin their two weeks of regrowth. Whatever had been skimmed became food.

If there had been more people, the process would have been much faster—up to ten trays a day would have been skimmed. But then, there would have been more waste to fertilize the trays, so their regrowth would have been faster.

And then there were the nonrenewable trace minerals that had to be bled into the system when they grew too depleted. It was a delicate balance but it could last centuries as long as the machinery was well tended and gravity or acceleration didn't shift beyond the tolerances.

In addition, there was the herb garden to look out for. This was not so automatic as life support, and without it their food would have been a nasty-tasting paste on nasty-tasting flat-breads. Carlotta had appointed that task to herself, too, as soon as Father could no longer get to the garden. Besides, his hands were so large that he could hardly manipulate the small leaves of the herbs. By the end of his time as ship's farmer, Father was uprooting as much as harvesting, and the garden had suffered.

The boys were content to leave all these maintenance

matters to Carlotta. The result, she noted with a mix of pride and bitterness, was that she was obliquely in the traditional role of women: cooking and housekeeping.

It took a willingness to repeat the same tasks over and over, and yet never become sloppy or lazy, and Carlotta wasn't sure she could trust such work to either of her brothers. She wasn't sure if it was species-wide gender differences or simply the personalities of the three of them, but for Ender, though he was capable of endless patience in pursuit of research, there always had to be a goal and a foreseeable end, while Sergeant had the attention span of, well, a six-year-old child.

In fact, Carlotta had a theory that Sergeant was the *most* human of the three of them—the most like an ordinary child. He was emotionally more volatile, more in need of constant stimulation, more desperate for action, change, *event*. Which was precisely what life on the ship never offered. There were no crises. Ender's research gave him results—usually negative—at a glacial pace, while Carlotta's maintenance work gave her no change at all, except in her own knowledge and mastery of the machinery and the theory behind everything on the ship.

Poor Sergeant. The most childlike of us, and therefore the one who suffers most from our utterly boring life. No wonder he keeps inventing fantasies of enemies and crises. Admittedly, killing Father was the most outrageous of his manufactured crises to date, and a deeply stupid and uncivilized act, but exactly the sort of thing that a child would think of.

And Ender punching him in the nose and half choking him had given Sergeant a blessed dose of crisis.

But the boy would heal, and his resentments and boredom and desperation would continue to fester and grow. What would he come up with next? Something terrible was going to happen someday. There simply weren't enough people on this ship to give variety to life.

"Sergeant needs a dog," said Carlotta.

Ender jumped. "What are you doing down here?"

"My work," said Carlotta. "What are you doing?"

"Samples," said Ender. "We've been working with viruses for gene splices for a long time, but there's some productive work being done with bacterial latency and chemical triggers. The biggest problem is changing every cell in the body at the same time, and keeping the immune system from rejecting itself after the change. We have some of the bacteria here in the trays and I'm going to try combining traits with some of our intestinal bacteria to see whether I can improve on their techniques."

He sounded so happy.

"You do know that Sergeant will never forget what happened the other day."

"You mean my beating the crap out of him?" said Ender. "I didn't expect him to forget. In fact, I'm counting on him remembering."

"It was surprise that let you beat him this time. You'll never surprise him again."

Ender sighed and made no answer.

"As I said," said Carlotta, "Sergeant needs a dog."

"Theoretically I suppose I could recapitulate all of evolutionary history and construct some small animal that he could amuse himself with. Unfortunately, it would take longer than our expected life span—and that's if I only make him something like a squid. If I have to create a chordate life-form, it would take even longer, and I'm not sure we could control the results."

"He needs something he can love and control at the same time," said Carlotta.

"I thought that's what you were for," said Ender.

"He doesn't control me."

"Really?" said Ender. "Apparently the puppet is unaware of the strings."

"I'm aware of everything you're aware of," said Carlotta. "What you see as strings, I see as my ongoing effort to try to keep Sergeant from going bonkers."

"I think we can count his plan to murder the Giant as a major failure of that effort."

"I wouldn't have let him do it," said Carlotta.

"When have you ever stopped him from doing anything?" The scorn in Ender's voice made her want to hurt him. Just a little. Perhaps a liver biopsy in his sleep—small wound, intense pain, quick healing.

"If you bothered to connect with anybody who isn't involved in genetic research hundreds of lightyears away, you'd know how many crazy plans I've kept him from acting on. The only reason you even knew about this one was that he kept it from me until he sprang it on you and you broke his face."

"It needed breaking," said Ender.

"All you did was convert yourself into the primary enemy. Watch your back, Ender."

"I've already diverted some of my attention to tracking what Sergeant is doing."

"You're so far behind him that whatever you're tracking, I can assure you it isn't Sergeant. Or rather, you'll see only what he wants you to see."

"But I can learn a lot from what he wants me to see. Carlotta, I'm in the middle of something and I'm holding a lot of things in my head right now. I'd like to postpone our little chat until a more convenient time."

"Sergeant needs something he can work on."

"Sergeant doesn't know how to work on anything that doesn't involve violent action or life-and-death struggle," said Ender.

"Which is what you and I are both working on, when you think about it," said Carlotta. "You're trying to fight off our genetically coded giantism before it puts us in the cargo hold ourselves, and I'm trying to make sure all the ship's systems keep working so we don't die from some malfunction or accident."

"My point exactly," said Ender. "Sergeant could work on really important things if he just put his mind to it. He's smart enough—I could bring him up to speed on the genetic research in a few months."

"He doesn't want to work for you, or for me. Sergeant is *not* a natural subordinate."

"Paranoid schizophrenics rarely are," said Ender.

"Don't ever say things like that," said Carlotta. "That's a real condition, which Sergeant does *not* have, and if you allow yourself to regard him that way—"

"Don't you have even a shred of a sense of humor?" asked Ender.

"There's nothing funny about what life on this ship is doing to Sergeant."

"If I don't laugh," said Ender, "I'd have to take him seriously, and that would distract me from my work."

"I was hoping you could help me come up with something that will help Sergeant bear his life. He suffers more from loneliness than you and I do. He's more like Father."

"The Giant and Sergeant? I never thought of that, but I think you might be right. Sergeant needs to be a street kid in constant danger of starving or getting killed. That would occupy him nicely. So what you really want is not a *dog* for Sergeant. More like a sabertooth tiger. Something that is stalking him constantly so that he can devote himself to fighting off genuine threats so he doesn't have to keep making them up."

"I was thinking more along the lines of a companion that extends his life beyond the boundaries of the ship."

"A dog on another world?" asked Ender.

"We have so much money, back in the human world, that it's just funny. That Graff man set up Father's finances so well that nobody back there has a clue just how wealthy we are."

"All the money we need would fit into my closed fist," said Ender.

"We have no use for it now," said Carlotta, "except I thought maybe we could buy something that Sergeant could tend in a sort of virtual way, through the ansible. Get somebody to implant something in some animal, maybe. On some colony world with a lot of wild country. Maybe a predator—your sabertooth joke might be a good idea."

Ender stopped gathering samples and thought for a moment. "He'd hate it coming as a gift from us. Or even as an idea we thought of. He'd think we were doing therapy on him, which would be true. He doesn't think he has a problem."

"I know," said Carlotta, though she hadn't really looked at it that way until Ender said it.

"You always say you know, but I don't think you knew any such thing," said Ender.

"I knew you'd say that," said Carlotta.

"All-wise, all-knowing, Carlotta the magnificent."

"About time you admitted it."

"There are bio-research labs on several worlds that are studying various xenofauna. I assume you're suggesting that I invent some kind of excuse for this to be a project of mine, which I would talk about with believable enthusiasm, so that Sergeant will think he's sneaking behind my back to get control of the creature and divert it to his own purposes."

"Something like that," said Carlotta, whose thinking hadn't

gone that far, since she had only come up with her plan as she said it to Ender. "There's no way I can do anything plausible along those lines, since my work is all here on the ship. But you have so many contacts by ansible."

"None of which have any idea that I'm a six-year-old antonine on a starship. I'm a different person to all of them, and because of the time differential I'm mostly doing data harvesting. None of them are relationships."

"I never thought they were."

"I just don't want you to think that I have some vast network of friends back in the human universe. If they found out who I am and where we are, we'd probably get a brief burst of attention from the media and then somebody might investigate our finances and somebody *else* will find a reason that it's illegal and take most of our money away from us."

"They can't find it," said Carlotta.

"Our software and our agents say they can't," said Ender. "Doesn't mean someone really resourceful can't do things that surprise them. But back to your point—I could do something like that. I don't think it would work, but it could be done and it might be worth trying. Do you want a pet, too?"

"Maybe just a link with a household robot somewhere, so I can watch someone else doing routine maintenance, day after day, year after year, so I can remind myself that machines have lives more interesting than mine."

"So you have as much self-pity as the rest of us," said Ender. "Don't we all suffer."

"You say that as if it's nothing," said Carlotta.

"Well, I don't *live* as if it were nothing. I'm so bored with the work I do that there are days when I just wish I could die along with the Giant."

"Do you know why the Giant doesn't want to die?" asked Carlotta.

"Because he loves us," said Ender, "and his work isn't done until he's pretty sure we have a chance at happiness. Whatever that is."

"He didn't have to love us, you know," said Carlotta. "You say that as if it were as natural as air."

Ender gestured at the life-support equipment all around him. "There's nothing natural about the air we breathe."

"Father is a good man. A noble man. A genuinely unselfish man."

"Wrong," said Ender. "Father is a feral child who came to admire a nun named Sister Carlotta and a slightly older boy named Ender Wiggin, and he wanted to be as good as he imagined them to be, so he bent his whole life to trying to pretend to be a real boy, and he's continuing to act out that script, because he's afraid that if he ever stops, he'll find out that he's still that same starving scavenger that stayed alive somehow on the streets of Rotterdam."

Carlotta laughed. "It doesn't occur to you that maybe it was the role of the feral child that was forced onto him, and the good man in our cargo hold is the real Julian Delphiki?"

"Does it matter? We're all feral children, and by 'we' I mean the entire human race and all of its variants. We've only just started to evolve into creatures that actually *like* and *need* civilization. We all have to suppress the aggressive alpha male and the savagely protective mother so that we can live together in close proximity."

"As we do on this ship," said Carlotta.

"I'll look for a pet for Sergeant."

"And for you," said Carlotta. "And me. And who knows? Maybe Father would thrive if he had some life outside this ship."

"That's a lot of bandwidth, to keep us all playing with animals on other planets."

"We can afford to pay for it," said Carlotta.

"I'll look into it," said Ender.

"Pretend that it matters," said Carlotta, "and that there's some urgency to it."

Ender said nothing more. He closed the lid on his last sample and left life support.

Carlotta was already finished with her readings. As usual, everything was working fine.

What routine, boring, lonely job was next? She hadn't checked the tracking software for a while. Weeks? Days? At least days. She closed up the floor panel over the gravitational field sensors and made her way to the elevator shaft.

When she first stepped onto the platform, it was a small floor under her feet. But as it moved upward, it passed into a flux zone, where she felt herself falling in every direction. She was used to it, though it still gave her a bit of an adrenaline rush as her body felt the usual momentary panic. The limbic node deep in her brain didn't understand that she no longer lived in a tree, no longer had to panic when she felt herself to be falling.

She kept her grip on the handle of the elevator and soon she came into the zone that kept Father's gravity oriented so that life support was toward the rear of the ship and not the bottom. In this gravity zone, the elevator shaft ran along the bottom of the ship—the keel, to use the nautical analogy—so that the cargo hold where Father lived was above her, and she was lying on her back, clinging to the handle as the elevator slid her forward. It was easy enough to hold on—Father's gravity was about like the Moon's, a tenth of what it was on Earth.

Ender was in the lower lab when she got there. It took her a couple of steps to move fully into the zone of Earth-normal gravity that the ship maintained in the forward compartments, where Father couldn't go anyway. Ender didn't look up—he was busy inserting his samples into various bits of equipment, some of them for freezing, some to be worked with right away. He had no time for her.

She envied him his sense of urgency. Unlike Sergeant's crisis, Ender's urgency was real enough—the deadlines loomed. Carlotta didn't believe for a moment that there was any chance of saving Father's life, but there was some hope for the three children, and Ender never lost track of that. In her heart, she knew that Ender was the only one of the children engaged in work that was truly important to them all. But he and Father were so immersed in it, had such a firm grasp on the state of the research, that she despaired of ever learning it well enough to be a colleague of theirs, an equal. She would always be the latecomer.

And yet she would drop all her work if they called for her, asked her to do any task, however menial. Here, tend to this while we do the real work—she wouldn't mind. But they never called for her help.

Wordlessly she passed Ender and climbed up into the upper lab. She sat down at the terminal for the tracking computer, brought up the holocharts, and began going through all the star systems that fell anywhere near their future path, starting with the stars they were just about to pass and working forward. The computer was looking for the arrangement of mass in each system in order to estimate how the gravitator would have to adjust its lensing.

It was on the fortieth star she looked at—one that was still several months in their future, but would come fairly near to them—that the computer pointed out an anomaly. There was an object that was being tracked as belonging to that star system, but according to the computer report, the object's mass kept changing.

That was impossible, of course, a mere artifact of the data. The mass didn't change, that's simply how it was reported. What was actually happening was that the object was not moving on a path that was predictable in relation with the known masses of the star and its larger planets. So the software kept adjusting the estimate of the object's mass to make it conform to its most recent movements.

It wasn't an "object" at all. It was using its own power to move on a path it chose itself, independent of the gravity of the star and its planets.

Carlotta told the software to regard the object as a starship.

Immediately she got a very different report of its past movements. The ship now had a constant mass—more than a thousand times more massive than the *Herodotus*. But the trajectory now made perfect sense. The ship was slowing down as it entered the star system. It was heading, not toward the star, but toward a rocky planet in the goldilocks zone.

Even the largest human colony ships were not so large, but they would have homed in on exactly that kind of planet. If the *Herodotus* were on a planet-scouting mission, that planet would have set off all the appropriate alarms. As it was, *Herodotus* routinely sent all the astronomical data it collected by ansible to the keepers of the master charts. Originally they were maintained by the International Fleet, but in recent centuries Starways Congress oversaw the constant updates.

The preliminary report *Herodotus* already sent had tagged the planet as having 1.2 gees of mass. In the goldilocks zone that meant it would definitely have an atmosphere, though, having held on to more of its hydrogen than Earth had, and lacking a twin planet like Earth's Moon, the composition of the atmosphere could not yet be predicted. As they got nearer in the next quarter century or so, Earth time, more information about the atmospherics would be collected and transmitted.

But Carlotta didn't care much about the planet. Planets were of no use to them because Father couldn't stand even half a gee, let alone 1.2. The fact that the alien ship was approaching it suggested that the atmosphere was attractive to whatever species the ship belonged to. But what mattered to *Herodotus* was the existence of the alien ship.

A starfaring species could not navigate through space without having instruments that would detect *Herodotus* as it passed by. The ramscoop and the plasma emissions were potentially dangerous to the alien ship and it might feel threatened, even though they were not on a collision trajectory.

Since the alien ship was slowing to approach a planet, Carlotta had no way of guessing whether the alien ship itself, or perhaps a smaller craft it carried inside it, had the speed to accelerate and match that of *Herodotus*.

They had several choices, now that she knew it was an alien ship. The *Herodotus* could turn aside slightly to avoid passing so near to the star system. This would not conceal their passage from the alien ship, but it would make it less likely that the aliens would feel any need to intercept them; their plasma emissions and mass collection would have no effect on any object reasonably construed as being a part of that star system.

But turning, however slightly, would require a significant slowing of the *Herodotus*. Objects traveling as close to light-speed as they were going simply could not turn. They would have to slow to less than eighty percent of lightspeed to bend their path even slightly; to make a turn of a degree or more, they would have to halve their velocity.

That would return them to the normal flow of time. The relativistic effects of near-lightspeed flight were not noticeable at lower speeds. That meant that genetic research in the human worlds would stop proceeding by leaps and bounds, relative to the *Herodotus,* but would plod along at the rate of at most two days per day, and probably less.

Would that matter? Nobody in the human worlds was working directly on Anton's Key anymore, anyway—only Father and Ender were doing that, and their work would not be slowed at all by a change in the ship's velocity. There might be some breakthrough in related research that was postponed for a while, but in more than four centuries, all such breakthroughs had been incremental at best. Interesting lines of research had opened up, but nothing truly vital had happened.

But Carlotta knew they were not limited to these two choices—continue at near-lightspeed in a straight line, or slow down enough to bend their course and then return to lightspeed as quickly as possible. There was a third choice. They could stop and meet the alien ship.

Dangerous. Potentially fatal. The human race had encountered only one alien species, ever, and had fought a war of extinction with them. According to a story told by the writer of *The Hive Queen* under the pseudonym "Speaker for the Dead," the Formics had not meant to wipe out the human race at all. But Carlotta wasn't buying it—it was easy to impute benign motives to an alien species that no longer existed.

So to slow down and meet this alien species was extremely dangerous—potentially lethal. The first Formic colony ship to enter Earth's solar system had been lethal. Both the early encounters out in the Kuiper belt and then the asteroid belt, and then the landing on Earth when the Formics tried to replace Earth's biota with their own, had killed thousands of humans. The war to save Earth had been a close-fought thing and the outcome had by no means been certain until the very end.

Formic technology had been more advanced than human tech, but there were gaps in the Formic mindset that humans exploited to defeat that first colonizing effort. By the time the International Fleet had reached all the Formic colony worlds, the technologies had become about even, except that humans had the molecular disruption field used in the ramscoops. Weaponized, the M.D. field was used to utterly destroy the Formic home world and, with it, all the Hive Queens.

What if *this* group of aliens had a technology as deadly to humans as the M.D. field had been to the Formics? Even if the technologies were more balanced, what if they were more malicious and relentless than the Formics had been?

The trouble was, it was too late to avoid meeting them. No matter what the *Herodotus* did, it would be detected—and its plasma path could be followed back till it disappeared. And since their flight had been straight as an arrow since they reached near-lightspeed, all the aliens would have to do to find the human home world was keep on going straight along the path marked by the *Herodotus*'s plasma emission trail even after the trail itself petered out.

The Giant and his children had a mission of their own—to stay at lightspeed while they worked to save their own variant on the human species. To save their own lives, if they could.

But what was the point, if the rest of the human race got wiped out in the meanwhile?

It would be far more useful to slow down and *stop,* not turn, so that they could discover as much as possible about this alien ship and its inhabitants. Using the ansible, they could report every speck of information they found—right up to the moment when the aliens destroyed them. The human race would then have time to make whatever preparations might be possible to meet these aliens when they followed the *Herodotus*'s trail back to Earth.

And there was always the chance that this alien species would have weaker technology than the *Herodotus.* Maybe they would be friendly. Maybe they would be downright worshipful.

No matter what, however, it was highly likely, in Carlotta's view at least, that the whole human race might have cause to be grateful to this little ship of antonines—or leguminotes, to follow Ender's little joke on Father's name. For if the human race could pick their first ambassadors to this new alien species, they could hardly do better than to choose the great warrior Julian Delphiki and his three astonishingly brilliant children. If any humans were a match for these aliens, it would be the doomed geniuses on this lonely little ship.

And it would give Sergeant something useful to occupy his time instead of plotting ways to kill Father—or whoever his enemy might be today.

Carlotta sent a signal to Ender and Sergeant. COME WITH ME TO TALK TO THE GIANT. SOMETHING IMPORTANT HAS COME UP. Then she copied the pertinent charts and reports to Father's holotop.

CHAPTER 4

Strangers Are Enemies

If it had been the Giant or Ender who called him, Cincinnatus might have ignored the summons. But he had nothing against Carlotta. She had respect enough for him not to waste his time. Ender and the Giant both assumed that whatever Sergeant was doing, it was worthless and therefore interruptible.

The cargo hold had always been the Giant's sleeping quarters, but Sergeant remembered the days when the Giant used to venture out into the labs and the helm. But only a year or so into the voyage, the Giant had grown too large even for the passages especially redesigned to accommodate his bulk. Cincinnatus remembered how sad it had made him, when the Giant became a prisoner in the cargo hold.

The last time Sergeant had been in here, he had been in pain from Ender's treacherous attack. Now the pain was gone and most of the symptoms had faded. Ender was now acting as nonchalant as if the incident had never happened. To him, it was probably forgotten already, too trivial to be worth thinking about.

But Cincinnatus thought about it all the time. The rage and shame of it still burned. He had to do something to make that pain go away, but he had no idea what. He certainly wasn't going to attack one of his sibs—that road led to the death of their new species before it had a fair chance to thrive. Ender might regard Cincinnatus's genes as disposable, but Cincinnatus knew that Ender was the best of them, the one whose genes were most vital to pass on to another generation. No matter how angry he might get, Cincinnatus did not lose track of what mattered.

At Carlotta's request, the Giant had linked his holotop to the big holodisplay, and now she pointed out the movement of an alien ship in a star system they were approaching.

He did not need Carlotta to point out their choices.

"Of course we're going to stop and try to communicate with them," said Cincinnatus. "We have no other choice. We can't leave a potential threat behind us without investigating it."

The others nodded. A group this bright didn't need discussion when the options were obvious.

"There's no reason for Ender to stop working on the genetics problem," said the Giant. "We're pursuing an interesting path that involves bacterial latency. Carlotta can manage deceleration, approach, and communications."

Cincinnatus felt his normal despair. As usual, no one could think of anything for him to do.

Carlotta, bless her little heart, took pity on him. He hated that. He didn't need to have his shame put into words. "What about Sergeant?"

The Giant looked at her as if she were an idiot. "He's going to arm the *Herodotus* so we're ready to turn this alien ship into dust if the need arises."

Just like that. For the first time in his life, Cincinnatus mattered. The Giant had a use for him.

Ender was skeptical, of course. "We don't want to go in guns blazing."

The Giant sighed, and now Ender got the are-you-really-this-dim look. "Andrew, sometimes I think you forget that each of you is exactly as intelligent as the others. Cincinnatus isn't going to use any weapons against an enemy whose capabilities we don't yet know. And even when we know them, he won't initiate hostilities. We don't need a war. We need an assessment. But if they want a fight, we have to be so ready that only a vastly superior technology could possibly kill or capture us."

Cincinnatus didn't have to say a thing. He had a job. An important one. And more to the point, he had the Giant's trust.

Enough trust that over the next few weeks, the Giant studied all of Cincinnatus's proposals and, with a few pointers and suggestions, approved them. Carlotta helped him put a small-scale M.D. field on the front of the Puppy, to act as a shield and, potentially, a weapon. Cincinnatus put in the hours of delicate work to weaponize the small atmospheric probes, designing them to cause several different levels of damage. It was vital to have an arsenal that could respond at the appropriate level. Total destruction was the least desirable option. How many alien races were they likely to meet on this voyage? It would be very nice to have something left to study, even if they had to kill everybody. Turning the aliens and their ship into a cloud of undifferentiated atoms was only the very last resort.

This was what Cincinnatus had trained himself for. It had seemed obvious to him from the start of his self-education. The Giant had survived on the streets of Rotterdam, finding ways to protect himself against enemies far larger and more capable than himself through a combination of cleverness, ruthlessness, and well-placed trust. Then, when Sister Carlotta found him, the Giant had gone to Battle School and become the very best at everything.

Cincinnatus had gone over the transcripts of the great battles that the Giant had taken part in under the command of Ender Wiggin, and again and again he saw that the Giant was the best. Wiggin had clearly understood this, relying on the Giant to take the most difficult assignments and trusting his counsel.

One brother was named for Andrew Wiggin. So be it—the Giant had loved him and served him well. The Giant called his daughter Carlotta, after the nun who rescued him, saw his value, and sent him off to war. But Cincinnatus was not named for someone out of the Giant's own past. Cincinnatus was named for the great Roman general who saved his country and then set down his power and returned to the farm to live out his life in peace.

That was what the Giant dreamed of—that's what this voyage was to him. An attempt to end his life in peace, to devote himself to saving the lives of his children.

To Cincinnatus, it was as clear an assignment as he could imagine. You are the soldier, the Giant was saying to him. You will follow my path to war. I have set down my military life; I give it to you.

So Cincinnatus relentlessly studied war, everything about war, from weaponry to tactics, from strategy to logistics. Every period, every battle, every general good or bad. He saw everything through the lens of war. He made himself ready.

And what did he get for it? The nickname "Sergeant," as if he were a mere noncom, never to be a commander.

But Cincinnatus bore the name and their disdain. He persisted in his path, reassuring himself that the Giant suffered worse abuse as the smallest child on the streets of Rotterdam and later, the smallest in Battle School. The Giant is testing me. I will show him that nothing bends me and certainly nothing breaks me.

The Giant consulted with the other two all the time, Ender about genetics, Carlotta about the ship. Cincinnatus was left to himself. He had despaired. He had tried to decipher, from the silence, what the Giant wanted of him. He had finally reached the conclusion that the Giant did not believe that it was possible to reverse Anton's Key. The Giant had failed in this last assignment. Like a Roman who failed in a great endeavor, there was nothing to do but sit in a bath and open a vein. Except that was not a soldier's way. A great soldier like the Giant would have another soldier put a sword through him and die as if in battle.

That's how it had seemed to Cincinnatus. But apparently he was wrong.

How could I be anything but wrong? he had cried out silently to the Giant. You never talked to me, you never told me what you wanted, I followed your path so closely that I could repeat every battle you ever fought from memory. But you left me to guess. You left me without any hint that you valued me or my work. You left me as alone as you were on the streets of the city.

When Ender bloodied his nose and damaged his throat—and could have killed him—Cincinnatus despaired. He felt like the prodigal son, who had claimed his inheritance and wasted it, and now was a mere servant in the Giant's house.

Only then, at the lowest point in his wasted young life, did the enemy appear on the far horizon. Then the Giant looked to his military heir and anointed him. Of course he is the one who will create our weapons! Of course he is the one who will prepare for war.

And Cincinnatus was ready. He had already planned how to weaponize practically everything on the ship. He had created the programs that would aim the plasma exhaust ports

to fry anything that approached the *Herodotus*. He had created programs to turn the ramscoop into a true ram that
would create a molecular disruption field to consume anything they came near. Cincinnatus had long since penetrated
all the data banks of the old International Fleet and the new
Starways Congress, and he was confident that if the need
came, he could defeat, one on one, any warship that the
human race could bring against him.

For he had always assumed that their greatest danger would
eventually come from humans who had decided that the leguminotes must be obliterated before they could supplant
Homo sapiens as the dominant life-form in the universe.

Instead it was an alien ship, and Cincinnatus had the Giant's trust as they decelerated to meet it. He should have felt
exultant, vindicated.

All he felt was relief and a little bitterness: Finally! And you
couldn't give me a hint that you needed a warrior son till now?

The relief and the bitterness quickly faded, however, and
now he had to face the realization that all he felt, day after
day, was a growing dread. No, not dread anymore. Raw fear,
that's what he felt. All his military study and planning had
been theoretical or historical. This was real.

If Cincinnatus did not do well, they all could die. If he
was too quick to use lethal force, he could bring on devastating retaliation; but if he delayed too long, a preemptive strike
by the enemy could destroy them with his weapons unused.
If he could not deal with unexpected enemy tactics on the fly,
they could die.

The Giant had always had the luxury of never having the full weight of command on his shoulders. Always there was Ender above him, or, later, Peter the Hegemon. Cincinnatus had the Giant, but the Giant had retired to his farm. The Giant was slow, and the stress of battle might overtax his heart. He might die. Cincinnatus had to prepare to fight alone to keep his brother and sister—his kin and his kind—alive.

When Ender made a mistake or followed a dead end, he just sighed and started again. Nothing lost but time.

But if Cincinnatus made a mistake, they might all be dead.

There were no trial runs. There were no games and tests. How could there be? When the Giant was in Battle School, the Formics were known. There was something to train for. But these new aliens—nothing was known. How could he train himself?

Cincinnatus found himself freezing up. He would be in the middle of a task and suddenly he would realize that he had done absolutely nothing for a half hour, an hour at a time. Instead his mind had kept racing through imaginary scenarios, always disastrous, always his fault. He would choke, he would freeze, he would panic and leave his sibs at the mercy of the enemy.

They were all counting on him, and from what they could see he was completely ready. The ship was outfitted for war, the software was tested and it worked perfectly. What they could not know was that inside his own head, Cincinnatus was crazy with fear.

I'll just tell them. I'll tell the Giant. I can't do this. I'm not your heir. I'm a sorry mistake. A failure. If it comes to war, you can't count on me to do anything at all.

He made the resolution over and over. He went to the Giant to tell him. Instead they talked over old battles. Why did you do this? Why did Ender Wiggin do that?

The Giant seemed to enjoy this. "The thing about Ender Wiggin was that he understood the enemy. The boys he fought against in Battle School, and the Formics themselves. He didn't know he was fighting the Formics, of course. He thought his opponent was Mazer Rackham, the one human being who had figured out the Hive Queens and used his knowledge to win the Second Formic War. So he fought Mazer Rackham as if he were a Hive Queen, and he believed Rackham was simply doing a superb job of faking the Formic way of war. So Ender tried to understand, not Mazer Rackham himself, but the Formics he was supposedly simulating."

"You were doing it too, weren't you?" asked Cincinnatus.

"No," said the Giant. "I was young then. I hated the enemy, I let my fear of the enemy drive me. What will he do, where will he move, what *can* he do, I must be ready to counter it. And I was very, very good. Very quick. Very creative. But Ender didn't think like that at all. He was thinking: What does the enemy want and need? How can I give them what they need, in such a way as to leave them vulnerable? How can I take away the enemy's will or capacity to fight? It's a different mindset."

"So why didn't you adopt that mindset?" asked Cincinnatus.

"I didn't know that's what Ender was doing. We were close—I was his best friend, and he was my *only* friend, your mother and I only tolerated each other in those days. But I didn't realize that he was doing something so profoundly different from what I was doing. I just thought his ideas, his orders came from pure genius. Or sometimes I thought his orders were insane, but it always worked, so afterward I called it brilliance."

"Why couldn't you think the way he did?"

"Because Ender knew how to love. I'm not talking about warm gooey emotions—though I didn't have those, either. I'm talking about putting yourself inside someone else and embracing their needs, understanding what they hunger for, and also what will actually be good for them. Understanding them better than they understand themselves. Like a mother who can tell when her child is sleepy even as the child absolutely denies that he's sleepy at all. He did that with his opponents. He saw them whole and true. And then he helped them discover the truth about themselves—that they weren't warriors. They didn't have the talent for it. He revealed to them that war was not their right path. Which was always true. War isn't the right path. If you love war, you'll fail at it, compared to someone like Ender who hates it so much that he'll do anything to win and put an end to it."

"You hate war to win it. You love your enemy to destroy him. I don't like paradoxes, they always feel as though somebody's trying to trick me."

"Usually they're just tricking themselves. But these aren't

really paradoxes. Someone who thinks he loves war is always wrong, because war destroys everything it touches. It unbuilds things. So when war can't be avoided, you fight in such a way as to reveal to the enemy how war is destroying him. When he finally sees it, he stops."

"Except that what Ender did was kill the enemy. Which works even better."

"No," said the Giant. "He wasn't aiming to kill. Remember, when he fought the Hive Queens he thought it was all training. He thought he was being tested by Mazer Rackham. So his goal was to expose to his teacher how destructive the testing process was. He fought as if he were fighting the Formics, but he was only ruthless within the simulation."

"He killed that boy in Battle School."

"He defended himself. Brutally, thoroughly. But murder was not his goal. He just wanted to show Bonzo that the war he insisted on fighting was destructive. He actually loved the boy. He admired his pride, his love of honor. He was trying to save him from his own destructiveness."

"I think you were the better commander."

"I was quicker than Ender. I was more ruthless." The Giant sighed. "But in battle after battle, I saw that Ender's way was the right one. And when I finally came to understand what he was doing, I tried. I just . . . didn't have the capacity to love my enemy. I understood Achilles well enough, but I didn't love him. I only feared him. Until the very end. But I had no choice but to kill him—that's what I understood. Achilles wasn't Bonzo. Achilles would never stop because someone showed him how destructive his wars were. Destruction was his *point*. He loved destruction. He was truly evil."

"What would Ender have done with him, then?"

"What I did. He would have killed him. Or tried. Achilles was smart and quick. He might have beaten Ender."

"But he couldn't beat you."

"I don't know about 'couldn't.' He *didn't* beat me."

Time after time during the conversation, Cincinnatus wanted to say, Were you afraid? I'm so afraid.

But he didn't say it. He talked, he listened, and he went back to the growing terror of preparing for a war he wasn't competent to fight.

He began to have nightmares. Vids of the Formics replayed in his mind, always tearing apart Ender or Carlotta or the Giant, as they screamed, "Sergeant! Help me! Save me, Sergeant!" And in the nightmare, he stood there with powerful weapons in his hands and he could not aim them, could not fire, could only stand and watch his family die.

The three of them bunked together in the upper lab, but when the nightmares began, Cincinnatus began sleeping in the Puppy, or in some other place in the ship, wherever he could curl up and catch a few hours of sleep before the dreams began.

He checked the weapons again and again, knowing that they worked fine; it was the soldier who was going to misfire.

So it was that when they began to get visuals from the tiny drones they sent on ahead of the *Herodotus,* Cincinnatus was already so terrified he could hardly breathe. He could not believe the others didn't notice. But they didn't. They kept deferring to him as they discussed possible strategies. And when the visuals began coming back and the sheer size of the monster starship became clear to them, they openly showed their fear—nervous laughter, lame jokes, outright declarations of awe and dread. But Cincinnatus showed them nothing, and they continued to rely on him.

The odd thing was that even though he was absolutely consumed with his own fear, the analytical part of Cincinnatus's brain didn't freeze up at all.

"I see no sign that the bogey has spotted our drones," Cincinnatus said. "In fact, I see no sign that they're doing any kind of recon on the planet, even though they're in geosynchronous orbit around it."

"Maybe they have instruments that don't have to penetrate the atmosphere," said Carlotta. "We do, after all."

"We can determine the oxygen content and so we know that it's a plant-dominated world," said Cincinnatus. "But if we were going to settle there, we'd be sending drones to pick up samples of the biota to determine the chemistry of life to see if it's compatible with us."

The Giant hummed a long low "Ummmmmm" and said, "The Formics didn't have to do that because when they colonized, they had this gas that broke down all life-forms into a protoplasmic goo. Their strategy was to get rid of the local flora and fauna and replace it with fast-growing flora of their own."

"So when the Formics came to Earth, they didn't probe or test at all?" asked Carlotta.

"Not as far as we could tell," said Cincinnatus. "I've been going over all that during the past couple of months and the Formics didn't do any of the things we would have expected. Now we understand why, but at the time we had no idea of their mission."

"You say 'we' as if you were there," said Ender.

"We humans. We military people," said Cincinnatus. "The way you say 'we' about scientists in general."

"So are you saying that these aliens are like the Formics?" asked Carlotta.

"No," said Cincinnatus.

"How could they be?" asked Ender, sounding impatient as if Carlotta's question had been dumb. "Think how different the Formics were from the human race. These aliens are bound to be completely different from *either* the Formics *or* us."

The Giant spoke again. "That's not what Cincinnatus meant."

Ender and Carlotta looked at Cincinnatus. "Well, what *did* you mean?"

Cincinnatus looked at the Giant. "What did you think I meant?"

"Just say it," said the Giant. "You don't need my approval first."

But of course that implied that he already *had* the Giant's approval.

"What I think," said Cincinnatus, "is that this ship isn't *like* the Formics. It *is* the Formics."

Carlotta and Ender were so surprised that Ender laughed

and Carlotta even let out a single derisive hoot. "The Formics are all dead."

Cincinnatus shrugged. It didn't matter whether they believed him or not. He might be wrong anyway.

"Help them," said the Giant.

"That ship isn't emitting any kind of radio waves. It has no drones, no probes. The engines only fired enough to get the ship into orbit around the rock. Then nothing. Would that even be possible in a human ship?"

"We never thought it was human," said Ender.

"Whoever is on that ship doesn't use electromagnetic waves for communication."

"So they have ansibles," said Carlotta.

"It's more than that," said Cincinnatus. "It looks like a Formic ship. Not the ones that came to Earth, but the same aesthetic is at work here."

"There's no aesthetic at all," said Carlotta.

"That's the Formic look. No attempt at grace or proportion. Look at all the openings. Could adult humans use those? They're low and wide. Perfect for Formic workers to scurry out. Just like the doors in the surface of the Formic colony ships. The colony expedition they sent to Earth was a new model. Smaller and leaner than this one. Also faster. Not as close to lightspeed as the *Herodotus,* but near enough to get relativistic benefits. But this ship—do you see anything that could possibly cope with relativistic speeds?"

Carlotta blushed. "I didn't even think of that. No. The shielding is stone, and no ramscoop. It has to carry enough fuel to accelerate that massive slab of stone and then decelerate it at the end of the journey. This is a slowship."

"It's practically a moon," said Ender.

"During their first wave of colonization, the Formics must have sent out ships like this," said Cincinnatus. "Huge because they had to maintain an ecosystem for decades of flight, not just a few years. Stone shielding to survive collisions with rocks, not radiation. It must have been ships like this that founded their earliest colonies."

"So how long has this one been traveling?"

"At ten percent of lightspeed—they might have enough fuel for that, don't you think, Carlotta?"

She shrugged. "Probably."

"They might have been going for seven hundred years, maybe even a thousand. Look at how pitted and cratered the shield is. How many collisions does that represent?"

"That's a long time to maintain a sealed ecosystem," said Carlotta.

"If it really is a Formic ship," said Cincinnatus, "and it really has been going for seven or eight or ten centuries, anything could have happened. A disease. Running out of unrecoverable trace elements. I think maybe they got to their original destination centuries ago, but it was uninhabitable so they went on, looking for another world. This might be the first one they found."

Carlotta shook her head. "When they came to Earth, the Formics went right down to the planet surface and started remaking it. Here they're doing nothing. I think they're dead in there."

"Then how did it get into geosynchronous orbit? The Formics never developed computers, because they had the brains of all the workers for data storage and processing. They had no automatic systems that we know of. Somebody detected this planet and brought the ship in."

"So why are they inert?" asked Ender.

"Because they saw us," said Cincinnatus.

Ender scoffed. "Come on, when they came to Earth our ships were swarming everywhere, from the Kuiper Belt on in!"

"But to them, our ships were nothing," said Cincinnatus. "Slow. They had relativistic starships by then and we had never left the solar system. Now, though, what did we just show these aliens? A starship that cuts nearer the speed of light than the Formics ever managed, and there they are in an old, prerelativistic ark. They don't dare go about their business. They're waiting to see what we plan to do."

The Giant spoke up. "At least we have to assume that's what they're doing."

Cincinnatus felt a little thrill of triumph. Probably the Giant had worked all this out just as he had—and probably faster. But he had assumed Cincinnatus had it worked out exactly right, and that the others hadn't.

"So . . . what do we do?" asked Carlotta.

"No, we're not ready for that yet," said Cincinnatus. He saw that the Giant had a little trace of a smile. "Remember that the Formics communicate mind to mind. There has to be a Hive Queen in this ship, or there'd be no point in sending out a colony. So if she's like the Hive Queen that came to Earth, she's waiting for the Hive Queen on the *Herodotus* to communicate with her."

"No," said the Giant. "Close but you're missing something."

Cincinnatus felt the blush spread up from his neck. Yet he knew immediately what the Giant meant. "I forgot. Of course. This Hive Queen has to have been in communications with all the Hive Queens from the established colonies, from the home world. They knew she was out here and that she was going on to look for another planet. If she died and was replaced by a daughter, they'd know the daughter, too. Distance means nothing to them. So when this Hive Queen finds out we're human, she'll know that we killed all the other Hive Queens."

Ender nodded. "We're knee-deep in kuso, aren't we. She doesn't recognize our ship because it's a design no Hive Queen anywhere ever saw. So she thinks we might be aliens of a different species. But the moment she knows we're human, she'll think we're the most terrible, ruthless enemy she ever faced. She'll assume we plan to kill her."

"What else *could* she believe?" asked Carlotta.

"Unless," said the Giant.

"Unless what?" asked Carlotta.

Cincinnatus had no idea what he was thinking. "Maybe she doesn't know?"

"Don't guess," said the Giant. *"Think."*

It was Carlotta who came up with it. "The Speaker for the Dead."

"That's fiction," said Ender.

"Your scientist friends think it's fiction," said the Giant. "Millions of people believe that *The Hive Queen* is so true it's scripture."

"What do you know about it that we don't know?" asked Cincinnatus.

"I know who the Speaker for the Dead is," said the Giant. "Because he also wrote *The Hegemon*. They bind the two books together now, back in human space. I knew Peter Wiggin and I'll tell you, every word the Speaker for the Dead wrote about him in *The Hegemon* was true. And every word about your mother. All true. He was just as accurate in writing *The Hive Queen*."

"How could he be?" asked Carlotta. "They were all dead."

"Apparently not all," said the Giant. "The Speaker for the Dead works from interviews."

"This is fantasy," said Ender.

"This from a six-year-old," said the Giant. "I'm more than three times your age and I know what I'm talking about. You don't. If you've read *The Hive Queen*, you know that they realized their mistake and deeply regretted having killed so many autonomous beings when they came to Earth. They assumed we were all workers and killing them means as much, morally speaking, as paring somebody else's fingernails. When they realized that each one of us was an independent, irreplaceable being, they retreated from their expansion into our space. Only they had no way to tell us, having no language, and we were deaf to their minds."

"Another reason why *The Hive Queen* has to be fiction," said Ender.

"So the war went on, and we killed them all," said the Giant. "The Hive Queen on this colony ship would have known every step of their decision. So when she finds out we're human she'll be scared of us, yes, she'd be insane not to be— but she may also be full of contrition and eager to show her peaceful intent."

"Or she might be bent on vengeance because we humans killed all her sisters even though they hadn't invaded Earth again," said Cincinnatus.

"That's a possibility, too," said the Giant. "And she's had a lot of time to think about what to do to humans if she runs into them. It might be abject fawning apology. It might be trickery to lure us into vulnerability. It might be a devastating attack the moment she knows what species we are."

"Or everybody on that ship might be dead," said Cincinnatus.

"You're forgetting that it got into a parked orbit," said Carlotta.

"I'm not forgetting anything," said Cincinnatus. "When you see something that looks dead, sometimes it's a trick, sometimes it's just silence, and sometimes the thing is dead."

"So here we are," said the Giant. "This colony ship could be brimful of angry Formic soldiers. It could be empty. It could contain a Hive Queen who wants nothing more than to be our friend."

"Well, what do we do? If it's really a Formic ship," said Carlotta, "we can't exactly call it with our ID code."

"I think there's no choice but to send an ambassador," said the Giant. "Or, if you prefer more accurate terminology, a spy."

"Who?" asked Ender. Cincinnatus was pleased to see that Ender didn't sound very eager.

"Well, I can't fit in the Puppy," said the Giant. "So I think it has to be one of you."

"I'll go," said Cincinnatus. "I'm the most prepared if things go wrong, and I'm the most expendable if things go *really* wrong."

Cincinnatus could see that Ender thought this was a terrible idea and Carlotta had her doubts.

But the Giant was fine with it. "Circle it and see what response you get," he said. "Land on the surface. If you can open a door, open it and invite inspection. Show your shape to them. Get out of there if it seems dangerous. And if you get no response, get out of there anyway. Opening a door is all. Don't go in, not alone. Do all you can that's not violent or threatening to try to get the inhabitants of the ship, whatever or whoever they are, to come out and start communicating. But don't go inside."

"I won't go inside," said Cincinnatus.

"He'll go inside," said Ender. "He practically has to. This is *Sergeant* we're talking about."

"You don't know me at all if you think I'd disobey an order," said Cincinnatus.

"He'll do exactly what needs doing," said the Giant. "And if he doesn't, he'll do no worse than either of you would do."

Ender and Carlotta had no answer to that. The Giant had spoken.

If only he had left it there.

"Besides," said the Giant, "Cincinnatus won't go inside because the thought of going in alone terrifies him."

He knows, thought Cincinnatus in despair. I could hide it from the sibs, but not from the Giant.

"I know it terrifies him," said the Giant, "because it terrifies me. Anybody who isn't terrified is too stupid to be trusted with anything so important."

He knows me, thought Cincinnatus. And he still trusts me. "So it's all right if I have to wash out my underwear when I come back?" he said.

"Please do," said the Giant. "*Before* you report to me."

CHAPTER 5

What Can't Be Done

Ender knew that Sergeant was piloting the Puppy around the alien spaceship. For a while he had even kept the image of it in a small corner of his holodisplay. But it kept distracting him from the genetic models that had just come through from a research team that they had funded through one of their foundations.

Alien ship—interesting. Maybe vital for the survival of the human race. Happening in real time, so that consequences of a mistake would be immediate and irreversible.

But what Ender was looking at was also immediate. He was looking at failure and death.

There was simply no way to reverse the portion of Anton's Key that caused the Giant and his children to keep growing at a steady pace throughout their lives without also reversing the process that allowed the continuous formation of new neural cells and structures at an accelerated pace.

Even if they could work out a mechanism for simultaneously changing the genetic molecules in every cell in their bodies—which was by no means likely, not without damage and loss—there was no simple one-step change in their DNA that would stop the giantism without also making them stupid.

Not stupid. Normal. But that was the unbearable alternative. Turning Anton's Key was the point of the experiment that had created the Giant and his murdered siblings in Volescu's illegal laboratory twenty-two years ago. But you could not turn or unturn only a portion of it. The segments of protein doing the two primary jobs could not be separated.

But a year ago, Ender had initiated research on another approach. Instead of reversing Anton's Key, or any portion of it, they could create the code for normal human growth patterns—rapid growth in early childhood, slowing down until another growth spurt at puberty, and then stasis for the rest of the life of the organism—and put it somewhere else.

The problem was that DNA was a blueprint, but the cell it controlled had to know how to read it. With Anton's Key turned, inserting code for normal growth patterns sent conflicting signals. They interfered with each other. The result was a buildup of garbage proteins in the cell with no collection and disposal mechanisms. It killed the cell in about a day.

And now Ender had confirmation that inserting code to

create garbage-collection routines also killed the proteins that Anton's Key required. There was no way that both jobs could take place in the nucleus of the cell at the same time.

All this research that they had sponsored had worked medical wonders for people suffering from many different genetic disorders. It had made it possible to create many enhancements and the effects were making a difference in the lives of millions of people. But they would never be able to do the one thing that the research had been intended to accomplish. They were on a starship headed to oblivion. They might as well go home and die.

Maybe Sergeant had been right. Maybe it would have been more merciful to cause the Giant to die when he still believed his children might be saved.

Ender checked again and again, looking for a flaw, some question they hadn't asked, some alternate explanation, some conceivable Rube Goldberg mechanism that could compensate for the cascade of errors that resulted from their elaborate processes.

But the law of unintended consequences was already overwhelming the whole project. Nothing in the human genome did just one thing. Every change they were introducing caused damage, and compensating for the damage caused more damage until it became so unlikely that they could remake the cell in a safe and productive way that it was not worth continuing.

"He's there," said Carlotta quietly.

"Leave me alone," said Ender.

"He's risking his life for us and you can't even pay attention? Do you hate him that much?"

Risking his life. What life? But Ender couldn't bring himself to say it.

Instead he swapped displays and there was the Puppy, attached to the surface of the alien ship near an apparent access point. Ender zoomed in and now the hovering drone was showing Sergeant emerging from the Puppy in a pressure suit. He was adhering to the surface using magnetics rather than the mini-gravitator onboard the Puppy, because they didn't want to risk lensing the gravity on the other side of the ship's surface—who knew what damage or chaos that might cause? Magnetics were awkward to work with and made movement slow and ponderous, but they would cause no damage.

Don't bother being so cautious, Sergeant, he wanted to say. If you lose your life now, it won't be much of a loss. It's not as if you have much of a life ahead of you, anyway.

That was ridiculous, Ender knew. It was disappointment turning into self-pity and despair. Not rational. Not helpful. So four insignificant people had an incurable disease that shortened their life span. That didn't mean they couldn't still be the founders of a short-lived, brilliant species. Maybe evolution could do what genetic manipulation couldn't—find mechanisms to extend their life span or minimize the giantism. Things weren't hopeless.

What mattered right now was Sergeant and the alien ship. Easy to say. Hard to turn off the despair.

Who would have thought that it was Sergeant, not Ender, who would turn out to be the useful one?

It took Sergeant only a few minutes to get the door open.

"It's like they don't use tools to open it," said Sergeant. He spoke softly and it was possible there was a tremor in his voice. Could Sergeant possibly be afraid? "Just one twist and it opened."

"How much air came out?" asked Carlotta.

"None," said Sergeant.

"Then maybe we're not inside the habitable zone," said Carlotta. "The atmosphere can't all have leaked out. There was no breach in the hull."

"Go inside," said Ender.

"No!" The voice of the Giant was urgent, immediate. "Do not go in."

"He can't tell anything from out there," said Ender. "Whether they're alive or not—if he doesn't find out now he'll just have to go back."

"But not alone," said the Giant. "He can't go inside alone."

"Come on back," said Carlotta, "and I'll go with you for backup."

"To see what kills me, you mean," said Sergeant. He laughed. Nervously?

"Send in a crawler," said the Giant.

"It's all wiring and sensors," said Sergeant. "This isn't an entrance to the ship, it's a maintenance access point. I'm going to try another door."

"Right," said the Giant. He sounded relieved.

"There's a likely spot just forward of your position about ten meters and three steps to the left," said Carlotta.

"What makes it likely?" asked Sergeant.

"It has a much more elaborate seal on it."

"Protecting the atmospheric integrity," said Sergeant.

"Seems likely."

"Take the Puppy," said the Giant.

"It's just a few steps," said Carlotta.

"He might need tools and he won't know which ones," said the Giant.

"And you want it nearby for a quick getaway," said Ender. "When the nasty aliens come staggering out to eat you."

"This is not a joke," said the Giant.

"I wasn't joking," said Ender. He felt a perverse, dark pleasure in provoking the Giant. Soon enough he'd have to tell him about the failure of these exhaustive tests. The death sentence. Why not a little jest under the gallows?

Words appeared in Ender's holodisplay. Apparently the Giant wanted to say something to him that the others wouldn't hear.

I KNOW WHAT YOU FOUND, said the words. IT WAS OBVIOUS BEFORE YOU BEGAN THIS ROUND OF TESTS.

Ender answered him aloud. "You might have told me."

I DID, said the words. YOU DIDN'T LISTEN.

"Told you what?" asked Carlotta. "What are you talking about?"

Ender typed his answer. SO YOU LET ME WASTE ALL THIS TIME.

She heard the typing. "Oh, a private conversation." She sounded disdainful. "Is the Giant telling you to shut up?"

IT WAS YOUR TIME, IF YOU WANTED TO WASTE IT.

"I wanted to succeed," said Ender.

YOU DID. NOW WE KNOW FOR SURE.

"Oh, so it's therapy," said Carlotta. "Can't you keep your mind on Sergeant? Do you have to talk about *yourself*? Are you having *feelings*?"

MAY I KILL CARLOTTA, PLEASE? Ender typed.

PERMISSION DENIED.

Sergeant was back in the Puppy and now it lifted off, just a bit, and slid across the surface toward the ingress that Carlotta had spotted. This one opened inward, and there was no obvious opening mechanism.

"Should I knock?" asked Sergeant. "It only opens from the inside."

"Any kind of lock or keypad or palmpad?" asked Carlotta.

"If it's Formics, they wouldn't need one," said Ender. "The Hive Queen would know they wanted to come in and make another worker open it from the inside."

"If I breach the seal," said Sergeant, "it might cause serious damage inside."

"It's a poor design that doesn't have an airlock," said Carlotta.

"The inside door might be open," said Sergeant. "We don't know what's going on in there."

"There might be fifty heavily armed soldiers waiting to blast you when you get the door open," said Ender.

SHUT UP.

Oh, the Giant was getting downright stern.

"I'm going to try levering it," said Sergeant. "Maybe it just pushes open."

"How likely is that?" asked Carlotta skeptically.

But Sergeant was already getting a pry bar from the Puppy's exterior tool rack. After a few minutes: "There's a little give, but I think the door isn't hinged. I think it slides."

"Better design," said Carlotta.

"So winch it open," said Ender. "Attach high-friction magnets and have the Puppy pull it."

"Which way?" asked Sergeant.

"Try both directions," said Carlotta.

It took ten minutes to set up the winch to pull the door one way. Then another ten minutes to change it to pull the other.

"This isn't working," said Sergeant.

Ender laughed. "Come on, you two. Think like a Formic! You're trying to open the door as if it were designed for a human to pass through. Formic tunnels are low and wide."

Sergeant muttered a few unpleasant words and then began to rerig the Puppy to pull the door in the direction they would have thought of as down.

It was slow, pulling against the drag of interior machinery, but it slid open.

"Puff of air this time," said Sergeant.

"But not a steady stream," said Carlotta.

"It's an airlock," Sergeant confirmed. "Good call, Carlotta."

Oh, so Carlotta got praise for finding the doorway, but not

a word of thanks to Ender for figuring out which way it opened. Typical.

"Go inside," said Ender.

He waited for the Giant to balk, but there was no counter-manding order.

Sergeant stood above the airlock entrance, doing nothing.

"Go in," said Ender.

"I'm scanning first," said Sergeant.

"If anything was in there, it would have come out with that air puff," said Ender.

Sergeant knelt by the door, pried up his magnetic feet, and lowered himself into the airlock. "Empty," he said at once. They could all see as much in the box in the display that showed the visual from Sergeant's helmet.

"How hard to open the inner door?" asked Carlotta.

"There's a lever," said Sergeant. "I don't know if it's electrical or mechanical. Big for the one, small for the other."

"Try it and see," said Ender.

"No," said the Giant. "That would breach atmosphere."

"So close the outer door first," said Ender.

Silence. They all knew: That would cut off Sergeant's escape route to the Puppy.

"I don't like it," said the Giant.

"Won't learn anything until I do it," said Sergeant. Again, his voice might have quavered a little.

The outer door slid shut.

"That one was electrical so the inner one probably is, too," said Sergeant. "I didn't damage the mechanism by forcing it."

"Or when you try to open it, you'll find out that you did," said Ender.

I'M ABOUT TO SHUT DOWN YOUR STATION.

Ender got up and walked over to sit beside Carlotta. "The Giant doesn't like my ideas," he said.

"Neither do I," said Carlotta.

"I'm opening it," said Sergeant. There was no loss of signal quality through the hull.

The visual from Sergeant's helmet showed almost nothing, even when Carlotta enlarged it to fill the holospace.

"Switch on a light," said Ender.

"Light forward," said Sergeant, sounding annoyed. Didn't he like Ender making obvious suggestions? Poor boy.

The visual now showed a low tunnel, with tunnels branching off in a couple of directions.

"Nobody there to greet you," said Carlotta. "They're all dead."

"Or they laid a trap," said Ender. "Go on in and see."

The entire display on Carlotta's computer went blank.

"Hey!" protested Carlotta.

"I warned you, Ender," said the Giant.

"Why punish *me*?" demanded Carlotta.

"Come on," said Ender. "They're dead, there's no danger."

"Wrong," said the Giant.

The display came back on. It was obvious that Sergeant had indeed slid into the low tunnel. It was tall enough that Sergeant was probably sitting up.

"There was motion a moment ago," said the Giant. "While you were wasting my time with your immature behavior."

"Ender's immature behavior," said Carlotta.

"Which you just matched," said the Giant. "Sergeant is in a dangerous place and you're wasting—"

Motion in the display. Lots of motion. A dozen small creatures emerging from side tunnels and beelining toward Sergeant.

"Get out of there," said the Giant.

At once the display jiggled and swiveled nauseatingly as Sergeant threw himself feetfirst back into the airlock.

The airlock door was half closed when two of the small creatures launched themselves through the door. One went for Sergeant's body, one for his helmet. It blocked at least one of the viewers, so the image lost its depth and went flat.

"Open the airlock!" shouted Carlotta.

Sergeant apparently had the presence of mind to remember where the lever was that controlled the outer door.

"Catch one and hold on to it," said Ender.

"You're a cold marubo," said Carlotta, not admiringly. But it was the right thing to do, and they both knew it.

The creature partially blocking the helmet's viewers blew away.

"I've got the one on my body," said Sergeant. "It's trying to eat through my suit."

"Get rid of it," said the Giant urgently.

"No, I'm holding it by the back now, away from me. It's just wriggling now. It's not sentient."

"How do you know?" asked the Giant.

"Because it's stupid," said Sergeant. "Quick but dumb, like a crab maybe."

"Get back to the Puppy," said the Giant.

"It's an air-breather," said Sergeant. "Or maybe it just likes atmospheric pressure, because it finally stopped wriggling."

"Flash frozen," said Ender. "Good way to gather specimens. Except for the destruction of every cell in its body."

"We'll still be able to tell a lot about it," said Carlotta. "When he gets it back here."

"You mean *I'll* be able to tell a lot about it," said Ender.

"Are you going to keep what you find a secret from us?" asked Sergeant. "Or will we all know?"

"He's just being a brat," said Carlotta. "I don't know what's got into him."

"He's jealous because I got to do something important for once," said Sergeant.

The words stung because they were more than a little bit true.

"It looks to me," said Ender, "as if the rats have taken over the ship."

"Oh, that's too much," said Carlotta, standing up and facing Ender in a rage. "Sergeant risked his life while you sat here all cozy and—"

"Carlotta, stand down," said the Giant's voice—over the

intercom this time, instead of coming through the computer. "Ender wasn't talking about *our* ship."

Carlotta instantly understood. "So you think that creature Sergeant caught is just . . . vermin?"

"Maybe it had some other function before," said Ender, "or they wouldn't have had them on their ship. But they're vermin now."

"Not the front line of defense?"

"Defense from what?" asked Ender. "Nothing about that ship suggests that they expected to encounter anybody but their own crew."

"So . . . vermin that are out of control because the sentient masters of the ship are all dead? What have they been living on?"

"I don't know yet," said Ender. "But this is a generation ship, not a relativistic one. There must be an internal ecology. These got loose in the ship."

"And you know this because . . ."

"Best guess," said Ender.

The Giant spoke again. "I'm glad to see your mind is finally engaged in the task at hand, Ender. Let's hold off on any more argument between the two of you until Sergeant gets back with the specimen."

"Have you already reported this to Starways Congress?" asked Sergeant, who was now inside the Puppy.

"It's automatic," said Carlotta.

"No it isn't," said the Giant. "I cut off all automatic reports the moment you spotted that ship, Carlotta."

"You're not telling them about this alien vessel?" asked Ender, surprised.

"I haven't even told them about this planet," said the Giant. "Nothing."

Carlotta was stunned. "Why not? If this alien vessel turns out to be hostile—"

"I have all the information stored. If they attack, I'll release it in a microburst from the ansible. Till then, it's our little secret."

"Is there some master plan going on here?" asked Ender. "Because if there is, maybe you should tell the rest of us, since you might stroke out and die at any time."

Carlotta slapped him. "Don't talk to him like that!"

"Keep your hands to yourself," said Ender savagely. "It's the truth, and the great Julian Delphiki can face any truth, can't you, Father?"

"There's a plan," said the Giant mildly. "No hitting, Carlotta. What are you, a five-year-old?"

"I'm six," said Carlotta lamely.

"Then act your age. Children are supposed to have learned the no-hitting rule by first grade."

Comparing her to ordinary schoolchildren was so insulting that Carlotta threw herself back down on her chair in a huff and brought up some meaningless maintenance reports.

"I think we should isolate the specimen," said Ender. "In case it carries some kind of alien disease."

"We already ascertained long ago that the Formic biology

is different enough from ours that their diseases don't affect us and vice versa."

"What if they came up with something new on this ship?" said Ender. "What if they died of a plague?"

"Then it won't affect us," said the Giant.

"What if this isn't the Formics?" asked Ender. "Then all your certainty goes out the window."

"It doesn't matter," said the Giant. "If it's carrying a microbe, it was just killed in the vacuum of space."

"There are viruses that can survive hard space," said Ender.

"We can't isolate it, Ender," said the Giant. "Residue is already all over Sergeant's pressure suit, and we don't have any means of isolating it anyway. We'll just take our chances. We never thought to equip this ship to deal with alien life-forms. We're not supposed to be exploring."

Ender knew the Giant was right. Ender had spoken the moment he thought of the possibility of disease, but hadn't thought any further than that. Sloppy. Embarrassing.

"Maybe we'll get lucky," said Ender, "and it'll be a plague that puts us all out of our misery."

"What's gotten *in*to you!" demanded Carlotta.

The Giant supplied the answer. "Ender just found out that there's no way to cure any of us of our little genetic self-destruct mechanism. Not without losing our intellectual prowess. And probably not even then. It can't be done."

"That's how to break it to them," said Ender. "Just blurt it out."

"I tried saying it to you gently a month ago," said the Giant, "and you didn't believe me."

Carlotta looked devastated. "So there's no hope."

"We'll all max out like the Giant," said Ender, "and then we'll die."

"You can put a lot of life into the next fifteen years," said the Giant. "I did."

"But you weren't cooped up in a starship a trillion kilometers from the nearest human beings," said Carlotta bitterly. "This isn't a life."

"Yes it is," said the Giant. "It's the one you have. Now get busy. Sergeant will be back in a minute, and we have to take this creature apart and analyze it. And keep this in mind, please: Somebody or something on that ship parked it in geosynchronous orbit. Until we know who or what did that, we have no idea what kind of danger or opportunity we've run into here."

CHAPTER 6

Show and Tell

When Bean was talking to them about science or history or engineering, he was hard-pressed to stay ahead of them. After all, Bean had spent his childhood learning only about the military, and his adult years—if they could be called that— actually leading troops in battle, or trying to stay one step ahead of Achilles. Solving real-world problems.

Here on the *Herodotus* he hadn't had that much of a head start on the children. With three of them pursuing their own lines of inquiry, it was all Bean could do to track what they were doing and learning while trying to do his own research along lines they weren't pursuing. Fortunately, the kids didn't think it was a race. They took time to play. Bean had no such luxury.

In all these intellectual pursuits, they spoke to him, and he spoke to them, as equals. They were learning together, teaching each other. And they felt that equality. They had no idea that they were children.

Calling him the Giant. Trying to hide from him. He understood the desire for privacy. He understood all the resentment—he agreed with it. How much had he hated Volescu when he finally understood just what his experiment had done to him?

They didn't understand how childish their reactions were. They felt like people, not *children*. Children never do understand their own childishness.

Then again, it's not as if children felt any emotions that adults didn't also feel. Children simply hadn't learned to hide their feelings as well as adults—they weren't as advanced at lying.

But their childishness amounted to more than that. They hadn't learned to *restrain* the influence their feelings had over their actions. Wasn't that the definition of adulthood? That you wanted one thing, but did another because you knew what was right and good, and wanted to do the right and the good more than you wanted to do what you wanted.

The long view, that's what children didn't have. Yet if he challenged the children on this point, they'd be baffled. They *took* the long view! They just didn't understand how "the long view" should apply to their immediate decisions.

And why should they? They'd learn moderation and self-control the way children always did—by bumping up against another child's immoderate, uncontrolled behavior. Meanwhile, though, Bean was afraid for them. Because he really didn't have long to live. He could feel the labored beating of his heart all the time; he could hardly sleep for how his heart kept lurching in his chest. He would die long before they were mature enough to restrain their impulses, long before they had learned how to get along.

They all thought they understood each other, and in many ways they did. What none of them was capable of understanding was their own character. They were so young, they still believed that the motive they knew about was the real reason for their actions. Adults could say, No, I won't say that, because I'm really just envious, there's nothing actually wrong with what he did. But the child wouldn't be aware of the envy, only the anger, so the criticism, the insult, the gibe would be spoken and the damage done. Trust broken.

They could not break trust with each other. They had to be able to count on each other or they had no future.

But if they could stay alive and keep working together, what a future they had! Bean could not begin to explain to them what he had in mind. Well, he could, of course, but it would take away the last of their childhood, and they would feel the oppression of knowing that their whole future was mapped out for them.

They had so little future, individually; but so much future, as the founders and builders of a new kind of human species.

But if they couldn't solve the problem of giantism and early death, their new species was fated to die just as they began to taste of adulthood. It would be a species trapped in perpetual childhood or, at best, adolescence. No, at *worst*. Volatile, rejecting roles forced on them by the needs of others—how could you found a new civilization based on the choices of adolescents? They rarely built anything, they just broke things.

Meanwhile, though, when they were interested in a problem, it was wonderful to watch how their minds worked. Tiny hands, small even for six-year-olds, grasping instruments, typing instructions, manipulating data in the holospace; and their minds, leaping to conclusions—right ones, usually—and grasping the implications of those ideas. Like being in the room with three Newtons.

Newtons and Einsteins who were selfish with the utter egotism of childhood. And it would always be thus.

Maybe failure is the best option. Maybe if we don't survive, maybe if the creatures on this ship destroy us, it will be better for the human race. Because what my children and I are creating here is a race of powerful children, filled with spite and fear and self-pity.

All I can do is help them see a standard of behavior better than the one that comes naturally to them. They'll either embrace it or not. I can't control it.

The convenient thing was that the children had their own self-chosen specialties. While Ender analyzed the half-exploded corpse of the alien rat-crab, Carlotta and Cincinnatus made repeated trips to the alien vessel in the Puppy. They did not return to the airlock. Instead, with Sergeant to protect her in case the ship started trying to defend itself and repel their tiny invasion, Carlotta opened all the maintenance hatches and took measurements and charted wiring and did whatever other engineering tasks were within her reach to figure out how the ship worked and, if possible, get some idea of what awaited them inside.

Both projects were getting fascinating results; Bean checked in on them every hour or so, and kept the audio channels on so that if they said anything, he could respond, just so they thought he was looking over their shoulders.

He wasn't, though. He had a project of his own. He was using the *Herodotus*'s instruments and drones to probe the planet they were orbiting.

It had an oxygen atmosphere. That meant that the bacterial revolution had taken place in the large oceans, and substantial plant life had moved onto the land. Scans in various locations showed no woody plants, mostly ground-huggers and ferns and fungi. Gravity of 1.2 gees on other worlds had not prevented the development of woody stems, leading to massive trunks, so the absence of wood on this world suggested that it was very young.

And there was no trace of animal life. Not even insects, not even worms, though that might be a function of the kinds of probes he was able to send.

That meant the planet was ripe for a takeover by a colony, with no worries about native animals; by a Starways Congress edict, plants were only required to be preserved as seeds, samples, and data, not in situ; animals changed everything, and large preserves, usually whole continents, had to be set apart to allow evolution to take its course.

What the children could not know was that the presence of the alien ship was mere happenstance, though if two ships were to meet in space, it was far, far more likely to happen near a habitable planet than anywhere else. Bean had already been heading here. As soon as the ship's sensors determined that there was a planet with an atmosphere in the goldilocks zone, he had bent the course of the ship ever so slightly to bring it to this location.

If the alien ship hadn't drawn them, Bean would have suggested that they stop and investigate for the sake of pure science. Because if one thing was clear to him, it was that these children could not spend their lives in this ship. They needed a world. They needed a project to engage them. They needed a place where they could create children in vitro and raise them as fast as the artificial wombs on the ship could produce them.

And here Carlotta thought she had a complete map and a complete inventory of everything on the ship.

But Petra and Bean had planned from the start that whether or not a cure was found for the fatal giantism, their brilliant children needed a home, a place where they could develop their new genotype in safety. An uncharted world.

If only Bean knew how much time he had. So far he was still managing to keep his body functioning, mostly by doing as little as possible with his hands and legs, just enough stimulation to keep his blood from pooling. Exercise could kill him; but so could indolence. He could not allow himself to die until he was sure that the children would stay.

He had figured that he could force them, if necessary, by crippling the ship. Now he wasn't sure that from the cargo hold he could do any damage Carlotta couldn't repair. So instead of trapping them, he would have to persuade them. And he couldn't do that without having plans he could lay out for them, plans that made sense and sounded attractive.

The alien ship changed everything. It represented a potential rival flora and fauna for them to contend with. If there were sentient beings aboard—sleeping colonists in stasis, awaiting arrival?—then it might be impossible for the children to grow up and raise families in safety.

Bean would not live long enough to find another planet. And if he died before they found a place where they could put down roots, chances were they would return to the Hundred Worlds and the opportunity would be lost. If they survived to adulthood, their genome would be regarded as defective. Chances are they would be forbidden to reproduce; at least that's how the laws were shaping up on the most civilized worlds.

Petra was long dead, but that didn't change Bean's promise to her. They had agreed that this was the best course for the antonine children. He was not going to change his mind now. But he couldn't stop the children from doing what they wanted. He could still shape their world to some degree by withholding information from them. But these weren't ordinary six-year-olds, ready to believe in magic and ghosts if an adult told them such stories. The only information he could be sure of keeping from them was the secret of his own plans and intentions. Yet he still had enough power over the ship, and over them, that his plans and intentions were the most important facts in their environment. Until he died.

After two days of study, Ender had his report ready, and so did Carlotta and Sergeant. They gathered in the cargo hold for show and tell.

Ender began it.

"This is a Formic ship," he said. "The proteins in the rat-crab are the complete set of Formic-world proteins, with no extras.

"But here's the odd thing. The DNA is almost identical to the Formics' own genome as gathered and recorded from the many corpses after the war. There are key differences, but they're localized. It's as if the Formics went for a kind of perverse neoteny—these rat-crabs seem to be a deliberate throwback to an earlier stage in Formic evolution, with these savage claws spliced on, and a hard carapace, which is only vestigial in the adult Formics."

Carlotta and Sergeant understood the implications at once. "So the Hive Queens can modify their own offspring," said Sergeant. "They decided that some of their babies would be those little monsters."

"I doubt they thought of them as their children anymore, if they ever did," said Carlotta. "When you have babies by the thousand, I bet the Hive Queens had no qualms about regarding a few of them as animals."

Bean refrained from the obvious comparison; they wouldn't have appreciated the jest.

"Any idea how they reproduce?" Carlotta asked Ender.

"This one was a female," said Ender. "It seemed fully capable of reproduction, but not on a large scale, and it had no egg developing inside it." He turned to Sergeant. "Did this one look any different from the others?"

"It looked *closer,* mostly," said Sergeant. "They were moving fast and coming right at me. All I had was a general impression of their size, but they seemed all the same."

"So maybe they were all female, like worker Formics," said Ender. "Or else both sexes were there, and sexual dimorphism is minimal, as in humans. What makes sense is that the Hive Queen doesn't want these creatures to have dominant queens of their own. So they're all capable of reproduction."

"They reproduce like rats," said Carlotta.

"There must be some limiting factor to their population," said Sergeant. "Or so the Hive Queen that created them intended. It might not have been the Hive Queen of this colony. They might have been developed long before and then reproduced naturally. The Formics might not even have remembered that these rat-crabs began as their kin."

"Do you think they're edible?" asked Carlotta. "Not to us, but . . ."

"They're meaty," said Ender. "You're right, this might be dinner on the hoof."

"So why give them those claws?" asked Sergeant.

"One crushing claw," said Ender. "It could snap any bone in *our* bodies like a cracker. Against the Giant here, I think they'd have to resort to using the other claw, which seems to be for grasping and tearing. They use the crusher to break things, then hold it while pulling and tearing."

"So it's a flesh-eater," said Bean.

"Or it eats a particularly tough kind of fruit or nut," said Ender. "We can't know until we see them in their habitat."

"Which right now is a huge starship," said Bean.

"My turn, then?" asked Carlotta.

"Are you done, Ender?" asked Bean.

"With the main stuff. Formic proteins, probably derived from the Formics themselves. Sergeant's the one who discovered they're dangerous and strong and quick. And I don't know how long a pressure suit would hold out against them."

"What kills them?" asked Sergeant.

"Anything. Their carapace doesn't protect them from anything stronger than teeth of smaller animals. They could crush each other, and they could be mashed by a fist-sized rock. So you tell *us* what weapons we should use to keep them at bay."

Sergeant nodded. "No bullets, not on a ship. I wondered if we could slow them down with a sedative spray."

"I'd have to have a living specimen to see what worked on them," said Ender. "But there are sedatives that have been used on specimens of Formic-world fauna from several of the colony worlds. I could whip up a cocktail of seds that have no effect on humans."

"I just don't want to go in killing them wholesale," said Sergeant. "Now that we know they're Formic-derived, it's not impossible that they're actually the ones piloting the ship."

"Brain's too small," said Ender.

"But they might have queens," said Sergeant. "Or some kind of collective mind that's smarter than any individual. I just don't think we should go in killing. I keep thinking of the old vids of the Formics during the Scouring of China, that vile fog that reduced living creatures to pools and piles of protoplasmic goo."

"So let's have several sedatives ready that can be delivered as a fog," said Bean. "And a good solid backup plan. An acid spray, for instance. Even if they're sentient or semisentient, if they come at us to kill us, we hit them first and leave them dead."

"Nature red in tooth and claw," said Carlotta.

"Don't get sentimental about creatures that want to kill us," said Sergeant.

"I wasn't sentimental," said Carlotta. "I approve of us getting our claws red, if that's what it takes to survive. We're all the Giant's children, aren't we? Not bloodthirsty, but not timid about killing when we have to. Not like that namby-pam that Ender was named for."

"You're talking about my friend," said Bean.

"Not ours," said Carlotta.

"If it came to that," said Bean, "you would have no truer

friend or stronger protector. But you'll never know because you'll never meet."

"You say that as if he were still alive," said Ender.

"Why do you assume he isn't?" asked Bean.

"Because it's been more than four centuries since the war."

"We're not the only ones who know how to use starflight to avoid aging at the same rate as the human race."

"But we're insane," said Sergeant. "Nobody in their right mind would do this."

"We're a new species struggling to survive," said Ender. "Why would the great Ender Wiggin become a wanderer?"

Bean didn't want to take the conversation any farther down that road. He'd had his suspicions ever since he read *The Hive Queen,* but he didn't want to put them into words, not while they were this close to an ancient Formic colony ship. "Carlotta?" he said. "What do we know about their ship?"

"It's definitely older tech. And it's Formic technology—no writing, but some major color coding. Lots of little motors, which is why they need to have all these maintenance hatches. Of course they had to eliminate a lot of doorage in later ships when they got up to relativistic speeds. This design wouldn't do at all.

"I think they build the ship in space by attaching everything to an asteroid they sculpted into the shape we're seeing. Probably most of the metal in the ship's frame and hull came from the iron and nickel and such in the rest of the asteroid. But it's not the impermeable alloy they used in the ships that invaded Earth back in the 2100s."

"They didn't need it yet," said Sergeant. "At only ten percent lightspeed."

"Right," said Carlotta. "I think this ship settles the argument." She was referring to a long-standing dispute among historians about the incredibly tough alloy that formed the shell around all the ships that the International Fleet fought against in the Formic Wars. Was the alloy developed as a defense against enemy attacks? That would imply that either Formics fought each other in space, or they had faced other species of aliens that humans had not yet encountered—or they came to Earth intending to go into combat against humans.

On the other hand, if the tougher-than-diamond shell was intended only to shield against radiation while traveling at near-lightspeed, it would suggest that the Formics had not come to Earth prepared for war; the impenetrability of their armor was simply coincidence.

This ark showed that Formics sent out their colony ships with no defenses against attack, only a primitive collision shielding at the front. The Formics turned out to be devastatingly formidable in war, but war was almost certainly not their intention when they came to Earth.

"Nice to know," said Bean. "Fortunately, the argument never mattered anyway. What else?"

"The huge pillars are structural—the whole strength of the ship is vertical rising out of the rock, like a huge skyscraper. But they're also hollow. Rocket engines, and they carry fuel. Not radioactive, lots of carbon traces. It must be a very efficient fuel because even if the rock contains huge fuel reservoirs, it's not as if they can ever take this thing down to a planetary surface to process whatever carbon-based fuel source they use."

"They don't need much fuel," said Bean. "It's a generation ship, so they don't have to accelerate much. Very slow burn until they reach cruising speed, and then nothing until deceleration."

"No way to guess how much fuel they have left. This planet might be their last hope, or just a casual visit to see if it might do. The machinery I looked at was aging but it works fine."

"Aging like a thousand years?" asked Bean.

"No. More like a hundred years. I think everything's been replaced again and again during the voyage. Plenty of indications that there's been a lot of servicing over the years. But none recently."

"Any firm dates?"

"Just estimates of wear and tear. There are structural pieces that have never been replaced, with pry marks and scrapes from multiple removals and reinstallments of the working parts. Lots of lubrication residue, but nothing recent."

"So we're looking at some kind of disaster that hit the ship maybe a century ago," said Sergeant. "Something that left the rat-crabs in charge."

"No maintenance," said Carlotta, "but there's still a pilot who understands how to put a ship into geosync."

"Anything else? Besides the pillars."

"I've been saving the best part. The huge barrel-shaped structure surrounded by the pillars is actually the housing of a giant rotating cylinder inside."

"So instead of spinning the whole ship, they spin a drum inside it? That's just crazy," said Ender.

"That's what I thought," said Carlotta. "But the Formics don't necessarily respond to weightlessness the way we do. Their skeletons are cartilaginous, not bony, so they can be replenished in a way our bones can't. I don't think the Formics spin the cylinder to create centrifugal gravity for themselves—it's for their life support."

"Plants," said Sergeant.

"In a space that size they could have trees. Really tall ones," said Ender.

"A rain forest," said Carlotta. "Or even multiple zones, so they can maintain a full range of useful bioforms. Food crops constantly reseeded. Maybe the rat-crabs are part of the harvesting system. A full-fledged ecotat—habitat for the entire biota to establish Formic life on the new world."

"Maybe their most invasive species," said Ender. "To get quick coverage."

"And of course it's generating oxygen for the ship in transit," said Carlotta.

"So what we do with our racks of trays under UV light, they're doing with a huge spinning drum."

"But the rest of the ship has no spin at all," said Carlotta. "We opened one maintenance door at a place where I could wriggle down and see the cylinder moving past. My estimate is that the spin would give them about three-fourths of a gee on the inner surface of the cylinder."

"Is that enough to overcome the pressure of acceleration?" asked Bean.

"Depends on how gradual the acceleration and deceleration are," said Carlotta. "And maybe they increase the spin during speed changes."

"I'm just thinking that it would save them having to move all the soil to the base of the cylinder whenever they accelerate," said Bean.

"But all the other rooms in the place would either have no gravity or their 'down' would be away from the mass of rock, in the direction of the rockets," said Carlotta.

"And the corridors," said Sergeant. "The Formics must have moved through them on all sixes. Because short as we are, I couldn't stand upright in their tunnels. An adult-size human would be on his belly and it would be hard to use a weapon."

"That's how the tunnels were on Eros," said Bean. "The Formics like their ceilings low."

"Well, it makes sense in weightless spaces," said Carlotta. "They're never out of reach of a wall or ceiling."

"But because the corridors are weightless," said Sergeant, "we can walk in them the other way. The tunnels are wide enough for two Formics to pass, so people as short as us can stand on the walls and be fully upright. We only have to jump over the entrances to the side tunnels."

"Can you jump with magnetics?" asked Bean.

"We'll set them as low as we can. We don't need to cling the way we do on the surface of a ship out in cold space. Just enough to keep our feet reaching for the floor."

"Good work, all of you," said Bean. "I know there's a lot more in your reports, and I've scanned your data as you collected it. I think we have all the useful information we're going to get from the outside, and from that lump of rab that Sergeant brought back."

"Rab," said Sergeant, giggling a little. "Rat-crab."

"Half a rabbit," said Carlotta.

" 'Rab' it is," said Ender. "Until they tell us what they call themselves."

"Now, when you go inside," said Bean, "you have to remember that Formic-based life-forms probably all have some degree of mental communication. Even if it's just a sharing of impulses and desires and warnings, they can tell each other what they need to know. So if any of the rabs notices you, they all know you're there. They might be smart enough to set ambushes. You have to be alert. And if it gets dangerous, get out. You are not replaceable. Do you understand me?"

Sergeant nodded, Carlotta gulped, and Ender looked bored.

"Ender," said Bean, "it looks to me as if you think you're not going in with the others."

That woke him up. "Me?"

"Three," said Bean. "I'd go myself, but you know my limitations."

"But I'm the biology guy," said Ender.

"Precisely why you need to go," said Bean. "Three for defense is the minimum anyway, but if you're there, you can learn things on the spot instead of waiting for them to bring things back for you to study."

"But I'm—I'm not trained for—"

Sergeant looked at him with contempt. "You think you're above getting your hands dirty."

"I was up to my elbows in rat-crab blood," said Ender.

"He didn't mean literally 'dirty,'" said Carlotta. "You think we're expendable and you're the irreplaceable one."

"Nobody's expendable," said Ender. "I just won't be much help."

"You beat *me*," said Sergeant dryly. "Don't pretend you're helpless."

"He's scared," said Bean. "That's all."

"I'm not a coward," said Ender coldly.

"We're all scared," said Carlotta.

"Terrified," said Sergeant. "When those rab bastards came at me I pooped my pressure suit. Nobody in his right mind *isn't* scared going into unknown territory facing fast-moving enemies and more potential enemies that you don't even know about."

"So why are we doing it?" asked Ender. "The ship is dead, it's not going to follow our trail back to Earth. The human race isn't in danger. Let's just make our report and move on."

That was what Bean most dreaded—the perfectly sensible

idea of getting out of there. But, knowing his children, he couldn't argue in favor of the course he wanted.

"Ender's right," said Bean. "We don't have to investigate anything more about this ship."

Sergeant and Carlotta seemed rather let down, but also relieved. They made no argument.

But Bean knew that Ender would keep talking.

"Fine then," said Ender. "Starways Congress can send a substantial force to come out here and explore this ship with actual trained *soldiers.*"

Sergeant seemed to bristle at this. "'Actual trained soldiers' won't be able to stand up in the corridors, not even sideways."

"They'll probably blow things up and kill everything," said Carlotta.

"By the time they get here there'll be nothing to kill anyway," said Ender. "Whatever went wrong a hundred years ago is probably still going on. So when they get here the whole ship might be dead and then it's perfectly safe."

Carlotta was outraged. "You think that's good? Right now there's *life* on that ship, and you think having it all die is good?"

"What do you think is going to happen to it?" asked Ender. "It's not as if we're going to transplant a Formic rain forest to the surface of this planet! It's just a museum."

"But it's a *living* museum," said Carlotta. "We need to make a record of everything while it's alive!"

"We have catalogues of Formic flora and fauna from the colony worlds," said Ender.

"But we never saw any rabs, did we," said Sergeant. "Did we even know that the Formics did this kind of genetic manipulation?"

"Yes," said Ender. "They had those metal-eating gold bugs and iron bugs on whatever that planet was. Shakespeare."

"One example," said Sergeant. "And you don't think it's worth going in to collect data while they're still maintaining some kind of ecosystem?"

"So we risk our lives for science?" asked Ender.

"Not for science," said Bean. "For survival."

"We don't need Formic biota to survive," said Ender.

Bean sighed. He had to tell them sometime before he died. Which could be an hour from now.

"It's true that we can't eat Formic plants and animals," said Bean, "not as they are."

They all caught the implication of his words. "You're thinking of adapting them to fit our protein needs?"

"Carbs are carbs," said Bean. "I've looked at the lipids from Ender's data on the rabs. I think they're digestible. Especially if we alter some of our intestinal bacteria to make a couple of simple transformations. So the problem really is the proteins."

"Why would we *want* to eat Formic proteins?" asked Carlotta, looking a little nauseated at the idea.

"Because we don't have a workable range of Earth crops and animals in the gene base here on the ship."

"I didn't know we had *any*," said Carlotta.

"And yet we do," said Bean. "Vital crops, a few key animals—honeybees for pollination, for instance. No meat animals, though. Rice and beans and maize and potatoes, but who knows how they'll do against competition from the native plants on this planet, or against the Formic flora in the ark?"

"Why would they *have* to competc?" asked Carlotta.

"He's planning for us to stay here," said Sergeant, his voice flat and expressionless.

"You were bringing us to this planet all along," said Ender.

"Once I saw it was in the goldilocks zone, I wanted to see," said Bean. "There's no cure. Puberty still comes at the normal age. So biological childhood takes up more than half your life, and I don't see how you could live long enough to ever see grandchildren. That means that any children you had would become parents without any parents from the pre- ceding generation to guide them."

"I'm going to throw up," said Carlotta. "I'm not letting ei- ther of them—"

"Of course not," said Bean. "In vitro. It's how you were conceived, my darlings. And there are several artificial wombs on board."

"Where!" demanded Carlotta.

"Where you can't sabotage them until you're mature enough to understand why this is your only hope. You can't save your own lives, I can't save you, that's the way it is. But the species can still survive because you're so *smart*. Even though sexual maturity comes late in our species' life span, intellectual ma- turity comes incredibly young. So you'll have years to teach your children. You can keep high levels of civilization, of technology, of history, of moral reasoning. You can survive."

"But we'll be dead," said Sergeant.

"Is life on this ship *life*?" asked Bean.

"I always thought we'd rejoin . . ." Ender let the words peter out.

"The human race," said Bean. "How do you think that's going to work out? I thrived because I was useful to them. They had a war to win, and if Ender Wiggin hadn't worked out as the commander they needed, I was the fallback. Then Peter the Hegemon needed me to fight Achilles. After that, I was a freak. A giant. The only reason they didn't fear me was because I was obviously going to die of giantism. And I didn't fit inside a tank or a jet cockpit anymore."

"So you're saying they'd kill us," said Sergeant.

"I don't know what they'd do. Study you maybe. But what they would not do is let you marry regular humans, or go around bearing children that were pure antonines."

"Leguminotes," said Ender. "We like *Homo leguminensis* better."

"I'm touched," said Bean. He said it flippantly, but it was true. They wanted to take some form of his name as their own. "My point is, you need a world of your own. You need to reproduce like crazy while you're still young, so you can teach your children everything. Give them a chance to hold their own when the rest of the human race finds this place."

"They must already be planning to come here," said Sergeant.

"I don't see how," said Bean. "I haven't told them anything about this place."

A moment of stunned silence, and then Ender laughed, and so did the others.

"You are such a kumo," said Ender. "Webs within webs. When were you going to tell us?"

"When I thought you might listen," said Bean. "Preferably before I died. But I have it all recorded just in case."

"I'm not going to do it," said Carlotta. "Even if we don't have sex—and we never, never, never will"—she looked fiercely at her brothers—"our *children* would have to have sex and that's disgusting!"

"No," said Bean. "Not if they're raised apart. There are enough wombs on the ship for you to each have a kid to raise in a separate habitation. You give them sibs every year. You know that within a couple of years they'll be smart enough to be helpful. You'll have three separate broods who did *not* grow up as siblings. They won't have the instinctive avoidance of mating within the immediate family."

"They'll still be siblings!" insisted Carlotta.

"Genetically sibs and half-sibs. But that's not what made you feel disgusted. Primates are only disgusted by the idea of mating with a partner that you experienced as a direct sibling raised by the same parent. If you don't know them that way, there's no disgust."

"So we lie to them," said Carlotta.

"Separate them," said Bean.

"Lie," said Sergeant.

Bean conceded the point. "That's half of what parenting *is*," said Bean. "Framing the world your children live in by telling them only what's good for them to know."

"Then you're a *brilliant* parent," said Ender. "Absolutely *brilliant*."

"Meaning that I'm a champion liar," said Bean. "Well, of course. It's not as if you don't spend half your lives lying to me and each other. It's what we invented language for. The poor Formics—they could never lie about anything."

"I'm not a liar!" insisted Carlotta.

"That's a lie," said Bean quietly. "But let's not call them lies. Call them stories. When things happen, we invent stories about them. About why they happened. That's all science is, and history—stories about why things happen or happened. They are never, *never* true—never complete and always at least a little bit wrong, and we know it. But they're true enough to be useful. I doubt our minds could even grasp the whole truth about anything—the nets of causality spread too wide to be held within a single mind. But the stories, the useful lies—we share those and pass them on and when we learn more we improve on them, or when we need different stories for new circumstances, we change them and pretend we always told them that way."

Ender buried his face in his hands. "It sounds so hard."

"Lying?" asked Sergeant.

"Raising children," said Ender. "The only parent we ever

really knew is *terrible* at it, and I don't see how we'll do any better."

"Thanks so much," said Bean. "For what it's worth, you are the worst kind of children to raise, and it's not as if I had much help."

"Oh, you did the best you could," said Ender. "That's the point. We've had five years with you on this ship, and what do we know? Not enough! Nothing! If you died tomorrow, we'd be hopelessly behind."

"You have the ansible. In the human worlds our little family is incredibly rich and we have agents working for us who don't even know we exist, but all that will continue after I'm dead. I've made sure you all know how to interface with them and I've trained you never to let on that you're not ordinary people somewhere in the Hundred Worlds."

"Oh," said Sergeant. "That's right. We're trained and practiced liars, after all."

"You'll have all the libraries in the world. What matters is what you learn how to *do*. Raise crops. Maintain a viable ecosystem. Don't poop in the drinking water. *Subsist* so well that you have surpluses so you can spend time teaching and learning, writing and creating. Maintaining technology and improving on it. You can do this. Or your children can, and their children."

"I'm a child *now*," said Sergeant, and suddenly there were tears on his face. "I can't be in *charge* of children."

"You've always tried to be in charge of *us*," said Ender, a little snidely.

"You aren't *mine*," said Sergeant. "I'm not *responsible* for you."

"And thus he stares adulthood in the face," said Bean. "Enough of this, my little ones. You can't absorb it all at once. And I can't make you do it anyway. But that's why I need you to get inside that Formic ship right away, so you can subdue it and get control of it and start adapting whatever life is in there so that it can coexist with plants and animals that you and your children can *eat*. And then you have to seed that world down there with whatever ecosystem you design and then go live in it. Do you have any idea how long that will take?"

"I don't think it's possible," said Ender. "I think the three of us will die up here, in the ark, while we're still preparing the plants and animals. I think it'll be our children or their children who actually seed the planet."

"*If* I agree to do it at all," said Carlotta. "I'm the only one with eggs, you know!"

"Come now," said Bean. "You know that the technology exists to turn any cell into a functioning ovum. Males have both X and Y. If you get stubborn, those wombs can be filled with babies that you had nothing to do with. So if you want to be a genetic dead end, that will be your choice. But you aren't going to use your ova as a tool, to be withheld or bestowed."

Carlotta was furious. She burst into tears. "So you're already planning to do it all without me!"

Bean reached out a hand, with great effort. He dared not touch her directly, for fear of hurting her. His hand was so huge, her body so small. But she embraced his hand and wept into it. She was angry, but she was also still his daughter. "I'm planning to allow all three of you the freedom to choose for yourselves, without depending on each other. But it will be so much better if you all choose to go ahead with the colony. Without fighting each other. For the sake of this wonderful new species, this cursed tribe of short-lived demigods."

"You make it sound heroic," said Sergeant.

"You are the Zeus and Apollo and Hera of your tribe," said Bean.

"Aphrodite," said Carlotta.

"Oh, right," said Ender. "This from the girl who says she'll never never never have sex!"

"Athena then," said Carlotta. "I don't want to be Hera."

Playacting. They were still children and they were going to put on a play.

But they were also going along with it. Or at least trying on the idea. Bean couldn't be sure what they'd end up deciding. But they hadn't broken into open revolt, not yet. He'd been able to sell the story as a great epic. In living it, though, there would be nothing heroic—just drudgery and difficulty and danger and failure and loss and grief, just like any other human lives.

"And remember this," said Bean. "You're still human. Teach your children that you're human. A different kind of human, but you're far closer to *Homo sapiens* than Neanderthals or

Australopithecines or Afarensids ever were. Don't let your children think of humans as the other. The enemy. As aliens. I beg you."

"They will," said Sergeant. "No matter what we do."

"Make it their religion," said Bean. "Make it their faith, that humans are to be blessed by whatever your children make of themselves. I didn't bring you here to destroy the human race, but to improve it."

"That's a noble story," said Ender. "But I think you just told us all about what such stories are worth, and how long they last."

"As long as they're useful," said Sergeant.

Silence for a long moment. Bean had nothing more to say, not right now. He had to give them the freedom to think about things on their own.

"Let's go invade an alien spaceship," said Sergeant at last.

"I'll go work on some kind of sedative fog," said Ender.

"I'm going to eat something based on human-friendly plants," said Carlotta, "and then I'm going to cry myself to sleep thinking of my poor babies getting raised by these cretins."

CHAPTER 7

Into the Ark

Cincinnatus made a point of testing Ender's sedative cocktail on himself before he agreed to carry it into the Formic ark.

Ender rolled his eyes. "You think I didn't test it on myself?"

"Just wanted to make sure the weapon wouldn't work against me," said Cincinnatus.

"I don't even know for sure if it'll work against the enemy," said Ender.

"Fine either way," said Carlotta. "I whipped up a batch of napalm."

"You aren't seriously thinking of bringing fire into the ark!"

Carlotta rolled *her* eyes at Cincinnatus. "He has no sense of humor."

"Not about weapons," said Ender. "What *are* you using as backup?"

Cincinnatus pointed to a shotgun leaning against the wall of *Herodotus*'s lander, which they had long since dubbed the Hound because it was so much bigger than the Puppy. They had never piloted it—never even detached it from the ship—so the Giant was going to pilot it remotely. The children would be going as passengers.

"A projectile weapon?" asked Ender.

"Plastic shot," said Cincinnatus. "It'll penetrate their carapaces and bounce around inside. Against the walls, they'll just rebound."

"And come back and hit us," said Ender.

Cincinnatus sighed. "Ender, while you were studying genes, I was studying weapons—and armor. Our helmets have visors and we'll be wearing gloves, jackets, and pants. I can't swear the rabs can't gnaw through, but it'll take time, and any plastic pellets that ricochet and hit our suits will just stop and either stick or drop. No harm either way."

"Very selective weapon," said Carlotta.

"The right tool for the job," said Cincinnatus. "My sister once taught me that principle."

"So what's our goal?" asked Ender.

"We have two," said Carlotta. "Besides staying alive and getting back safely."

"I know we have two goals," said Ender. "I just wanted to know the priority."

"We've got to find the pilot first," said Cincinnatus.

"Whoever parked the ark in orbit is the most likely source of danger. Only after we have control of the ark do we go into the ecotat and see what kind of biota is keeping the ark alive."

Ender nodded.

Cincinnatus was surprised and relieved that Ender didn't even seem interested in taking command. In fact, both of them were conceding leadership to Cincinnatus. Hard to believe that only a few weeks ago, they'd been fighting.

But it was also hard to believe that Cincinnatus had seriously proposed killing the Giant. Cincinnatus remembered clearly that he had been quite sincere in his proposal. What he couldn't do was reconstruct the arguments that he had used to persuade himself that it was the only course of action.

I was as irrational as any prince who takes it into his head to depose and kill his father the king. Absalom, Richard the Lionheart—they were doubtless as convinced of the rightness of their actions as I was. And just as stupid, too.

It was hunger for action. And now I've *got* action and I've got command and I'm terrified.

"Carlotta," said Cincinnatus, "you stay in the middle. I'm point and Ender is rear."

"Protect the girl?" asked Carlotta contemptuously.

"If there's anyone with a hope of understanding the internal layout of the ark, it's you," said Cincinnatus. "We'll all fight if we have to, but any surprise attack should hit one of us, not you, because you're the one who's going to tell us the likeliest direction to go to locate the helm of the ark—or to get us to safety."

Carlotta nodded. "Eh, makes sense. Thought for a second you were getting all boy-o on me."

"Not me," said Cincinnatus. "I respect your secret androgyny."

"As I respect yours," said Carlotta.

As they talked, they had been putting on their armor. Cincinnatus helped them fasten things properly—he had lasered these down to child size, so they fit pretty well, but the fastenings were a bit jury-rigged and counter-intuitive.

"I think we're ready, Father," said Cincinnatus.

The Giant's voice came over the cabin speakers. "Attach yourself to a wall and strap in. I don't want to have to worry about you bouncing around in there while I'm maneuvering."

"So you're planning to show off what a hotshot pilot you are?" asked Ender. Cincinnatus made sure that they were all leaning against the wall of the cabin as the walls extended grips to hold them firmly. The lander was designed to carry cargo—there were no seats. The walls were designed to restrain whatever was placed up against them, whether people or cargo.

"Eh," said the Giant. "It's been a while since I had a chance to fly a sweet machine like the Hound."

After the experience of bumping around in the Puppy, Cincinnatus was duly impressed with the Giant's piloting skills. The Hound detached and puffed free of the *Herodotus,* and then suddenly it was moving forward. There were no lurches, no abrupt changes of direction. One smooth parabola, a marvel of efficiency, and they were positioned over the still-open airlock of the ark.

From the belly of the Hound, a self-shaping tube extended and created a seal against the surface of the ark, completely surrounding the airlock door. The children watched on a holodisplay at the front of the cabin. They felt the sudden gust as air from the Hound puffed into the tube and the open airlock.

"The I.F. used to have these boarding tubes extend from the side of landing craft, so assault teams would go into the enemy ship standing up," said the Giant over the intercom. "But after Ender Wiggin taught us that the enemy's gate is down, all the newer launches had the tube in the bottom, so we dropped down onto the enemy ship."

"What's the point?" asked Cincinnatus. "In zero-gee, we can orient ourselves however we want."

"Humans tend to keep a residual orientation. Reflex. So you deliberately orient yourself in the most useful way. Why not have the equipment support that?"

"So the lasting result of Ender Wiggin's genius is that boarding tubes come out of the bottom instead of the sides?"

"That and the extermination of the Formics," said Bean. "And the safety of the human race, and a whole slew of unoccupied Formic colony worlds for the human race to occupy. I guess it didn't really amount to much. Not in the eyes of children who grew up in the universe that Ender Wiggin reshaped."

"Ender the Xenocide," murmured Ender.

"Say that again on my ship," said the Giant, "and I'll change your name."

Cincinnatus snickered. "I suggest 'Bob.' "

"It's not what *I* call him," said Ender.

"You just did," said the Giant.

"It's what the whole human race calls him now. Because of that book, *The Hive Queen*."

"The Speaker for the Dead really did a number on old Ender Wiggin's reputation," said Carlotta.

"We're connected," said the Giant. "When you get the inner airlock door open, command passes to Cincinnatus."

Carlotta dropped down the tube first and made sure the outer airlock could close behind them, in case some accident detached the tube from the ark's surface. She closed it and reopened it twice. Then she called and Cincinnatus and Ender dropped down the tube into the airlock, carrying their shotguns, with the spray packs on their backs and the nozzles attached to their wrists.

Cincinnatus switched on his helmet's display, and after a moment's recon, the helmet computer began to outline and label all the key features of the airlock. That was the easy part—Carlotta had already programmed in all the information from Cincinnatus's first foray. As they went farther into the ark, Carlotta would orally label whatever she saw that needed labeling, so that the helmets could create maps on the fly, and they would all see the same names for everything.

What Cincinnatus cared about was the heat and movement sensors that would tell him where to aim and how fast the target was coming at him.

Cincinnatus positioned himself in front of the inner air-lock door. He half expected a couple of dozen rabs to be positioned all around the door, waiting to pounce the moment it opened. That's what he would have done, if he'd been in charge of defending the ark.

Of course, that presupposed the ability to command the rabs. As Ender had pointed out, it was just as likely that the rabs were wild now, and posed as much of a danger to the pilot as to the children who were invading his ship. The pilot might be sealed off somewhere, and she might view Cincinnatus and his team as liberators.

I am the great god Quetzalcoatl, and I have returned.

"What?" asked Carlotta.

"I was being Cortez," said Cincinnatus. "Sorry my lips moved."

"Thought you were subvocalizing," said Carlotta. "My helmet tried to interpret your words and couldn't. 'I am the great god' was all it got."

"Quetzalcoatl," said Ender. "The flying serpent, returning to his people after long absence."

"With sedative spray and soft-shot guns," said Cincinnatus. "Open the door, please, Carlotta."

The door slid open.

Nothing moved.

Cincinnatus slipped into the corridor, orienting himself to stand upright in the narrow space. To Formics, he would seem to be sideways, standing on the wall. Not that it made any difference. He tested the feel of his magnetics and murmured, "Mags five."

The others gave the same command, tuning their boots to stick even less tightly to the "floor."

In the corner of Cincinnatus's display, his rear view showed that Ender had oriented himself in the opposite direction, so that what felt like a ceiling to Cincinnatus was Ender's floor. Cincinnatus's first impulse was to snipe at Ender for clowning around, but then he realized that it was smart not to have the same up and down. Anything that tried to drop down on Cincinnatus from above would seem to Ender to be coming up from the floor—much easier to see and shoot.

When Cincinnatus came here before, he had seen rabs almost immediately. Did it mean anything that they weren't showing up yet?

The Giant's voice murmured in his ear. "I assumed that the ecotat would have days the same length as the Formic home world. If your previous entry was at Formic noon, you're now coming in at midnight."

"If they're nocturnal then this is day, same benefit," said Ender softly.

"If they're dusk feeders then this is dawn," said Cincinnatus. "And we're iced."

"I don't see any yet," said Carlotta.

"We're all getting the same instrument feed," said Cincinnatus. "Let's talk only when there's something important to say. Goes for you, too, Mr. Giant."

"Fe fi fo," said the Giant.

"Fum," murmured all the children, echoing the old game from their infancy.

The corridor they were in ran around the perimeter of the ark. That meant it would lead back on itself. "So do we want a tunnel taking us toward the middle of the ark?" Cincinnatus asked Carlotta.

"There won't be any here," she said. "The ecotat cylinder is inside this section. Can't you feel it turning?"

"Only a slight vibration," said Ender. "I'm betting the rotation is friction-free at the perimeter."

"Cushion of air," said Cincinnatus.

"Lubricant fluid," said Carlotta. "Sealed in. Or trillions of ball bearing beads."

"Irrelevant," said Cincinnatus. "My fault for 'cushion of air.'"

They fell silent again.

"I think we want to go forward," said Carlotta. "The helm could be at the front or aft, but this was designed to protect a Hive Queen and she'd be near the rock."

"No," said Ender. "I mean yes, the Hive Queen would be at the point of maximum protection, but no, where she is has nothing to do with the helm."

Cincinnatus got it at once. The Hive Queen of this ship would have seen through the eyes of every Formic worker. She could be anywhere.

"Sorry, yes, right," said Carlotta. "Got to stop thinking like a human."

"Same question then," said Cincinnatus.

"The way the controls ran, it seemed to me they were piped toward the stern from forward. Reduplicated for redundancy, I assume a full set in each of the standpipes. And that puts the helm in the center, forward."

Cincinnatus thought back to where the airlock had been and which direction he had led them along the perimeter corridor. "So is that up from here?"

"As you're standing, yes," said Carlotta. "Down for Ender."

"Pick us a passage, Car," said Cincinnatus.

"I hate 'Car,' " she murmured.

"You hate 'Lotty' worse," Ender whispered.

"I can still hear you," said Cincinnatus. "You have a one-syllable name during this mission."

" 'Car' is too much like 'Sarge,' " said Ender. "She's 'Lot,' I think."

"Lot," said Carlotta.

"Shut up now please," said Cincinnatus.

They passed under two upward passages but Carlotta didn't tell them to go up. It wasn't until they came to a large opening to the left that she said, "This is one of the standpipes."

"Aren't those rocket tubes inside?" asked Cincinnatus.

"But all the controls run up between the standpipe and the hull," said Carlotta. "Let's at least take a look."

The passage was sealed off from the perimeter corridor—an airtight seal, so that a breach in the hull would not suck air from the passages that ran the length of the ship. It opened with a lever like the one at the airlock.

Inside, there was a crescent-shaped space. The desiccated corpses of four Formic workers were discarded like broken dolls, some of their limbs broken off and randomly strewn. Cincinnatus couldn't help a momentary recoil.

"I don't think they died here," said Ender almost at once. "They were probably thrust down here by the force of deceleration as the ark approached the planet. They were already completely dried up by then—all this breakage came recently, and they've been dead for a century."

"So they died when the Hive Queen died," said Cincinnatus.

"Presumably," said Ender. "That's what Formics do."

"The rabs didn't eat them," said Carlotta.

"Guess they can't work the levers," said Cincinnatus.

"Not smart enough to understand them," said Ender. "They're strong and dexterous enough."

Cincinnatus looked at the passage that rose upward. Unlike the perimeter tube, this corridor had ribs and pipes that could be used like a ladder. Made sense—when the ship was accelerating or decelerating, the Formics would need them because it would be a definite uphill climb.

For now, though, in zero-gee, Cincinnatus again picked a sideways orientation and swung himself up into the tube. Carlotta followed, and Ender once again came in upside down.

They passed several stations like the one they had entered through, but then there was another sealed door and on the other side, the tube began well over from the one they had just come through.

"Offset," Carlotta murmured. "So nothing can fall the whole length of the ship."

"How long *is* it, anyway?" asked Ender.

Nobody bothered answering him. They all knew that the Formic ship was about twelve hundred meters long from the point where the tubes entered the rock to the openings of the rocket tubes at the rear of the ship. The forward quarter of each standpipe was detached from the hull, which had a narrowing waist from there forward to the rock. That's when they'd leave the standpipe tube and move inward again.

The whole length of this standpipe had apparently been sealed off from the rabs. They ran into no more corpses, and no hostiles, either. But when they came out of the standpipe passage into another perimeter corridor, it was a different story.

The air was filled with debris, floating like dust motes in a beam of light. It took a moment to determine that they were body parts. The helmet's heat sensor showed Cincinnatus that there might be living creatures beyond the curve of the corridor in both directions, but none within line of sight.

Ender came through and began picking pieces out of the air to examine them.

"Bits of rab bodies, but also bits of other life-forms. Wings like insects. Really big ones. Lots of little skeletal bits, skin I don't recognize."

"Garbage bin?" asked Carlotta.

"Rab dining hall," said Ender. "Not tidy eaters. Formics would never have left a mess that interfered with visibility."

Cincinnatus's helmet alerted him. "Either they smell us or sense our heat," he said. "We've got company. Both directions."

Immediately Ender flipped himself to the "ceiling" and faced along the tube; sure that he was doing his job, Cincinnatus faced the other way. "Spray first, En, but don't be shy with the shotgun if they don't slow down. Lot, figure out where we go from here."

"Can we move in one direction or the other?" asked Carlotta. "I can't see any likely passages from here."

"My direction," said Cincinnatus. "En, stay close; Lot, can you tether him so you can tug him? Don't want any gaps opening."

He knew that Carlotta would obey, hooking a three-meter cable from her belt to Ender's. He had no time to check, anyway, because the rabs came hurtling through the debris, rebounding from wall to floor to ceiling, scattering a hailstorm of bones and shells and wings and skin bits as they came. It was like intertwining tornadoes coming up the corridor.

Up the corridor. All at once Cincinnatus understood how useful Ender Wiggin's "enemy's gate is down" doctrine could be. Cincinnatus dropped onto his back and then braced his feet against the walls, the narrow way, and shot the spray down between his legs.

The spray—if it worked on rabs at all—was supposed to be very quick. It shot out from the nozzle in a fine aerosol fog, but at such speed that it filled the corridor for at least ten meters ahead. The smell was very faint.

Naturally, the sedative fog did nothing to slow the rabs' forward progress; Cincinnatus had his shotgun in firing position at once, aiming downward between his legs, as he waited to see what condition the rabs were in when they arrived.

They were still bouncing off the walls, but now he could see it wasn't a controlled movement. Instead of always landing on legs, any part of their bodies might hit the wall, and they tumbled end over end instead of jaws first.

"Spray's working," said Cincinnatus.

"Eh," said Ender.

"So let's keep moving," said Carlotta.

Cincinnatus had a momentary flash of resentment—who's in command here, anyway?—but realized at once that she was right and he should already have given that order.

He reoriented himself so he could walk in the corridor again. Drugged-up rabs from Ender's direction pelted him in the back as rabs hit him in the front. The suits absorbed much of the shock, but not all of it. Not enough of it. There'd be some bruising, and when they hit Cincinnatus's face mask, the impact rocked his head back. He moved forward briskly, firing off a short burst of spray every ten meters or so. Ender didn't fire at all—they were moving into the residue of Cincinnatus's spray, leaving Ender's original burst of fog to guard the passage behind them.

Cincinnatus passed a large airtight door on the right, leading toward the center of the ark. He made a quiet bet that Carlotta would choose this one, because it wasn't open and therefore might be rab-free. Sure enough, she levered it open and there was no debris inside, though a good amount of it began osmoting through, along with fog.

"Next time wait till I'm covering you before you open a door," Cincinnatus said sternly.

"Sorry, next time, yes," said Carlotta. Cincinnatus pushed past her and scanned the corridor ahead. Empty. Nothing. No heat or motion ahead.

He saw Ender move through the door and Carlotta closed it. The amount of debris that had come through was relatively slight, and Cincinnatus led the way along this corridor at a brisk walk.

"Haven't killed anything yet," said Ender. "Unless bumping into walls kills them."

"And nothing followed us through the door?" asked Cincinnatus.

"Clear," said Ender.

"We've got a long hike to the center of the ship," said Carlotta.

After a short way, the corridor opened out into a huge sandwichlike chamber. Cincinnatus forced his mind to reorient to the way Formics would have seen the room. The space between floor and ceiling was no more than a meter, but both surfaces undulated. And both surfaces were pocked with indentations. Deep ones.

"Sleeping quarters," Carlotta guessed.

She had to be right. Each indentation was deep enough for a Formic worker to crawl in to sleep. The soft, organic surface would protect them from the stress of acceleration. Cincinnatus reached a hand inside and pressed against it. It broke. Once it might have been resilient, but it had dried out. Probably the Formics moistened their own cells when they slept, to keep them supple. But now the walls crumbled into flakes when pressed.

It was tough going. Their magnetics were useless, and when they tried to brace themselves against the floor or ceiling, they broke away. But Cincinnatus soon got the knack of applying only slight pressure with his hands to keep himself drifting along at a steady pace. He touched the bedstuff only when he had to deal with the undulations; otherwise he just floated. He checked and saw that the others were keeping up. Whether they imitated his technique or learned it on their own didn't matter. They were making good progress.

Some of the cells had Formic corpses in them. Most were empty.

"Where are we heading, Lot?" asked Cincinnatus. "This goes on forever."

"There's probably structure toward the hub. This tenement must hold hundreds and—"

"About three thousand," said Ender, "if it's the same all the way around. Minus a few for whatever's in the center."

Cincinnatus wasn't surprised that, out of danger for the moment, Ender was processing information about how the Formics lived rather than keeping his mind on-mission. But then, that *was* Ender's mission. When they weren't on combat alert, he was studying the lifeways of the organisms in the ark while Carlotta studied the machinery and floorplan. Cincinnatus remained alert, but there was no apparent danger.

The helmet kept him going in a straight line toward the center, showing him the way to go whenever he got off target while avoiding the undulations in the ceiling and floor. They got to a rather impressive speed, considering, so when a metal wall loomed into view, there was no way to brake himself. He could only flip himself around to land feetfirst, absorbing the shock with bended knees. The magnetics were set too low to hold him in place and he rebounded, though at a much lower speed.

"Mags at two hundred," said Cincinnatus. Meanwhile, he and Ender collided—Carlotta had narrowly missed him—and they made a mess of the surrounding Formic bed spaces while they waited for the mags to draw them toward the metal at the center. They were both covered in flaky bedstuff by the time they got their boots attached to the metal wall.

"Mags at five," Cincinnatus said, so he could move again.

The hub had regular openings, with no doors on them. Cincinnatus dropped through the first one when Carlotta gave the OK.

They found themselves in a long corridor running in the direction of the axis of the ship. This time the tube had tracks on what the Formics would consider to be the floor and the ceiling. It made sense—a cart would never stay on tracks that only ran along the floor. Something was hauled along these tracks—and regularly. Cincinnatus saw that the metal tracks were shiny with constant use.

"The trains are still running," Carlotta said.

As if on cue, Ender gave warning from the rear. "Press into the corners, here comes the train."

Cincinnatus dropped to the "floor" he had been walking on and stretched himself out. Moments later, a tram moved along the tracks, tension bars holding the wheels to both sets of tracks. The body of the tram was like a chicken-wire cage, bulging with some kind of organic material. Plants? No, they were writhing, pushing against the wire. But nothing was getting out.

Not rabs, not even rablike. These were soft-bodied creatures, more like slugs, but with wider bodies and a kind of hair. Or cilia. Caterpillars? Analogies to Earth fauna would probably be unproductive and misleading. Ender's job, anyway.

Cincinnatus followed the tram but did not try to keep up with it. The thing was automatic. The question was whether it would run in a loop or reverse direction and come back this way for another load.

It didn't come back, and after a while Cincinnatus came to a place where the tracks curved inward toward the center. Cincinnatus stayed with them, of course, and came up against the back of the tram, which was stopped exactly over an opening. A sickening odor was coming from the space where the opening led.

Through the chicken wire Cincinnatus could see that something was cleaning out the cage.

It was a rab.

But it ate nothing, just scraped out the last of the clinging slugs. Then the opening closed, the tube was dark again except for the light from Cincinnatus's helmet, and the tram moved along in the same direction instead of backtracking. So it was a loop. And the load had been delivered.

Cincinnatus gathered them around the place where the opening had been. There was no visible lever to open the door.

"What now, Lot?" asked Cincinnatus. "There was at least one rab on the other side, but it didn't eat the slugs, just pulled them out."

"Did it look like that's what the grabbing claw was designed for?" asked Ender.

"Not our concern right now, but . . . yes," said Cincinnatus. "Could be that this is the task the rabs were actually designed for."

"Meanwhile," said Carlotta, "I think we can trip the signal that tells the system that a tram is here, so the door will open. It's mechanical. Look, the wheel passes over a treadle and the pressure trips a switch." She looked at Cincinnatus. "Ready for me to open it?"

"Fog ready," Cincinnatus said to Ender. They got their nozzles into position to spray into the opening. "I warn you, it stinks in there," said Cincinnatus. "Now, Lot."

The door opened.

The stink hit them right away and got worse as they moved into the room, which was humid and hot.

A half-dozen rabs were gathered nearby, but they were busy herding the slugs along a metal ramp that sloped gently upward. One of them noticed Cincinnatus and turned to face him, but it didn't leap to the attack. On the contrary, it simply went back and flipped the lever that closed the door again. But by now Cincinnatus, Carlotta, and Ender were all inside the chamber.

No, not chamber. Cavern. Unlike the Formic workers' dormitory, this space had much higher ceilings—several meters, maybe five. But rising to it or descending from it like stalagmites and stalactites was a lot more of that organic material, only now it was spongy and resilient, and the indentations were far narrower.

The rabs pushed the slugs up the ramp toward the center of the cavern. There was a platform there, with a soft light aimed at it from several directions. The whole room was centered on that space.

The smell got worse the farther they moved along the ramp, but they also got more used to it. The helmets also started cleaning the air inside the visor, which helped a little.

The slugs stuck to the ramp and the rabs clung to the edges of the ramp. The mags kept the children standing upright.

"It's like a throne room," said Carlotta.

"These are egg chambers," said Ender. "This is the Hive Queen's chamber."

But there were no eggs. Instead, the closer they got to the platform at the center, the more the egg chambers were filled with a brown goo with streaks of green. Putrefaction. The slime of decay.

At the end of the ramp, the slugs were pushed onto the platform. But since it was already piled high with slugs, mostly dead ones, the new ones toppled off to the sides, plopping into the slime below the ramp. The slugs swam like eels, but there was nowhere to go, except slime-filled egg chambers.

"They're feeding the Queen," said Ender. "Only she isn't here."

By now Cincinnatus had reached the platform. He waded through slugs toward the center. At the focal point of the beams of light, a low wall kept any of the slugs from getting into a three-meter-wide circle in the exact center.

Within that wall, sprawled and curled across more of the organic material, was the gray, dried-up corpse of a winged creature that had to be at least the size of the Giant.

"She's here all right," said Cincinnatus. "But she isn't hungry."

CHAPTER 8

At the Helm

Carlotta hated the Hive Queen, dead as she was. The Hive Queens' ability to communicate so perfectly with their daughters meant that there was no need for any kind of communications system. The Hive Queen could pilot the ship from anywhere. The pilot could be anywhere, too, with no need for visuals or even instruments, because whatever the Hive Queen knew from any of her daughters was known by all the others.

Therefore Carlotta couldn't find the helm by tracing the wiring of an intercom system, or looking for radio signal sources. The helm did not have to be in a place where visuals were possible.

She stood over the Hive Queen's body while Ender took holoimages of the corpse. "Don't touch it," Ender said. "She'll crumble into dust."

"So I guess this means interrogation is out of the question," said Carlotta.

"Go ahead and ask her anything," said Sergeant.

Carlotta didn't feel like joking any longer. "Somebody piloted this boat, and it wasn't her. But I can't trace the communications system because there isn't one."

Ender was oblivious to their concerns. "I've got all the images I can and they're stored back on *Herodotus*. So I'm going to take a sample."

"What happened to 'crumble into dust'?" asked Sergeant.

"I'll be careful," said Ender.

"I guess he thought we'd kick our way through her," said Sergeant.

"I don't care about your rivalry, *boys,*" said Carlotta to Sergeant. "We've found the heart of the ship, and it's a pool of rotting corpses that were supposed to be the Queen's food."

"It's a system that's so resilient it keeps going even when the Queen is gone." Ender couldn't keep the admiration—no, the *pride*—out of his voice. As if he had designed the Hive Queen's system himself. "No robots, no computers, just animals bred to do a job."

"Like us," said Sergeant.

"The Giant was bred," said Ender. "We were born."

"Just a continuation of the experiment," said Sergeant. "Only our designer wasn't as good as the Hive Queen's."

Carlotta saw that Ender really did have a delicate touch—he lifted off sections of dried-up Hive Queen from various regions of the corpse, but never disturbed anything, or even pressed downward. Just nipped a bit, raising it as he did, and pushed it into self-sealing sample bags.

Then what Sergeant said registered with her, and she saw that it registered with Ender at the same time, because he raised his hand away from the corpse and got a thoughtful look.

"The Formics were really good at genetics," said Carlotta.

"But no lab," said Ender. "Not here, anyway. Or their lab was the Queen's own ovaries. By an act of will she could decide when to extrude an egg that would become a new queen. And presumably to create an egg that would become a rab instead of a worker."

"It can't have been reflexive," said Sergeant. "She had to plan what she was doing, at least when she was making rabs."

"And while she was doing that," said Carlotta, "who was piloting the ship?"

"She was," said Ender.

"And who was tending to the ecotat, and who was doing maintenance everywhere, and who was reporting to the other Hive Queens on other worlds?"

"She was," said Sergeant. "Hive Queens are smarter than we are."

"Multitasking is fine, but was she really seeing and hearing the sensory input of all her workers at the same time, equally well? Or did she concentrate her attention where it was needed? There has to be a limit to how far she could subdivide her attention."

"Why does there have to be a limit?" asked Ender.

"Pretend I'm as smart as you for a minute, and think with me, please," said Carlotta. "It's not as if the Formic workers have no brains. And look, she's dead, but this system goes on without her."

"It's not Formics, it's rabs," said Ender. "Sheepdogs."

"She could have had Formic workers do all these jobs, though, couldn't she? What was the advantage of creating a self-replicating species to do it for her?"

Sergeant and Ender now understood her point. "She can't subdivide her attention infinitely," said Sergeant. "She needs to have automatic tasks that go on without her having to think or decide anything."

"This was a mindlessly repetitive task," said Carlotta. "But doing maintenance on the ship required that you understand what you were doing. Did she have to simultaneously control each Formic worker doing every job? Or did they have independence once they knew what job to do?"

"You're saying that the individual Formic workers weren't just an extension of her mind," said Sergeant. "Not like hands and feet. More like perfectly obedient . . . children."

"Somebody piloted this ship," said Carlotta, "and she wasn't there to control them. What if some of the Formic workers survived her death? If she wasn't controlling every thought in their heads, if they had the independence to learn their job and do it even when the Queen wasn't paying attention, then when she died, they could go on."

"No," said Sergeant. "It makes sense, but we know that

every Formic worker died when the Hive Queens died. There were assault teams on some of the Formic planets when Wiggin killed the Hive Queens, and the human soldiers reported that all the Formics stopped fighting at once. Stopped running, stopped doing *anything*. They lay down and died."

"But they lay down," said Carlotta.

"Dropped," said Sergeant.

"I read the same reports," said Ender. "They lay down. Some of them had vital signs for as long as half an hour. So Carlotta's right. There were at least some body systems in the workers that kept going for at least a little while after the Hive Queens died."

"What if this Hive Queen, *knowing* she was going to die, gave some of her workers instructions to keep piloting the ship?" asked Carlotta.

The others nodded. "We can't know what mechanism makes the Formics die when the Queen does," said Ender. "Maybe there's an exception."

"Let's find the helm and see," said Sergeant.

"That's the problem," said Carlotta. "I don't know how to find it. Do we have to try every door in the place?"

"You're saying," said Sergeant, "that if the workers had some independent thought, and the Hive Queen wasn't constantly having to channel information from observer Formics to Formic pilots, then there might be data connections after all."

"Or the daughter who was serving as pilot at any given moment would have to be in a position where she could see.

At least dials, readouts. She had to know when she was exactly the right distance from the planet. And if the Hive Queen wasn't channeling that information to her constantly, there'd be instruments I could track."

"Why not just track the firing mechanisms of all the rockets?" asked Ender. "The pilot has direct control of those—that's how the ship is steered, so controlling them is what the pilot is *doing*."

"Because that's the most dangerous part of the ship," said Carlotta. "Tracing instrumentation isn't intrinsically dangerous. Tracing the firing mechanism of the rockets is. The pilot might be waiting right now for us to get near that system so she can burn us up."

It felt vaguely wrong to think of a female in connection with brutal violence. But all the Formics the human race had ever seen or known of were female, and they were as dangerous as they needed to be. What had Kipling said? The female of the species is more deadly than the male. True for Formics, that was certain.

"Anything that would kill us would damage the ship," Ender pointed out.

"They have redundancy built in everywhere. They can absorb some damage. We can't."

"So let's start the open-every-door approach and if we run into the data collection system we can trace the wiring," said Sergeant.

"This is a big ship," said Ender. "There are a lot of doors."

"But most of the ship is the cylinder of the ecotat," said Sergeant.

"It's more than a kilometer in diameter," said Ender. "The rabs are well behaved in here, but the feral ones will be in a lot of other places. Our supply of sedatives isn't infinite, and the effects wear off. I can just see this working out like a videogame where all the bad guys suddenly come back to life and pounce on you at once, game over."

Carlotta looked out over the sea of rot that surrounded her. "Home sweet home," she said. "I'm trying to see this the way she did, when she was alive. All these little holes were like wombs for her eggs. All these slugs were being herded here to feed her and feed her babies."

Ender pointed up. "Don't forget the ceiling."

Carlotta looked up. Lots of stringy protuberances hung down from the highest points. A few of them had melon-sized balls hanging from them.

"What's that?" Carlotta asked.

"Cocoons. I'm sure they're all dead, but I'm going to want to take one back to the lab to study, if I can," said Ender. "Everything that's on the floor has been contaminated with that bacterial soup of decay. But larvae that cocooned themselves might still have clean genetic material I can study."

"Not our highest priority," said Sergeant.

"But not our lowest, either," said Ender. "We obviously have time to stop and chat. So let's collect a sample or two before we leave the Room of Goo."

"You going to take a slug back? And the bacteria?" asked Sergeant.

"Already collected samples of those on the way in."

"You were supposed to be our rear guard, not a prancing naturalist," said Sergeant.

"Nothing attacked us from behind," said Ender. "Hive Queens aren't the only ones who can multitask."

"Boys," said Carlotta. "Is this how our whole lives are going to be? The two of you sniping at each other?"

"Let's get one thing clear," said Ender. "Only one person has been sniping and it wasn't me. I've followed every order without complaint; I've criticized nothing. It's Sergeant who's determined to catch me doing something wrong. But I'm not. Carlotta said it—the Hive Queens were expert geneticists, and they worked on their own genome to create the rabs. So what I collect here might teach us science that the human race hasn't developed on its own. It might save our lives."

"Might," said Sergeant.

"There's the sniping again," said Ender. "It isn't 'boys,' Carlotta, it's Sergeant."

"We have to find the pilot," said Sergeant, "and we're not splitting up."

"Fifteen minutes," said Ender. "You shoot down one of the cocoons and Carlotta and I will catch it."

"With what? Sedative fog? A *shotgun*?" Sergeant looked triumphant.

"With the laser cutter you hid in your belly pack," said Ender.

Carlotta hadn't noticed. Ender didn't miss much. "So you have a much more lethal weapon than *we* have, is that it, Sergeant?" she asked.

"I thought it was possible we might face a living Hive Queen," said Sergeant.

"But only you would have the power to kill it?" asked Ender.

"So much for you never sniping or criticizing," said Sergeant.

"Enough," said Carlotta. "The Giant is listening to everything we say. We're wasting time arguing about whether we have time to waste. We don't. But collecting a cocoon is not a waste, so let's just do it and then go on to look for the helm."

Both boys glowered, but they couldn't argue with her—the reminder that the Giant was listening helped still them.

"And here's where you're both so stupid it hurts," said Carlotta. "The illusion in here is so good that it fooled you both."

"What illusion?" asked Sergeant.

"The illusion of gravity," said Carlotta.

She watched in triumph as they realized: The cocoon wasn't going to drop when they cut it loose.

"But the other cocoons fell," said Ender lamely.

"During deceleration," said Carlotta. "The ship turned around and the rockets pushed upward to slow this big rock down. That's when the cocoons dropped."

"But all this liquid," said Sergeant. "It clings to the floor."

"It clings to the egg holes," said Carlotta. "It's not liquid, it's *goo*. Most of the voyage is in zero-gee. If the eggs and larvae need liquid to grow in, it has to be gelatinous so it stays put, or the Queen would be drowning in it."

Ender was, of course, extrapolating. "The Hive Queen needs an environment just like home," he said. "On a planet, the liquid might just be water, the larvae would climb to the ceiling to make their cocoons. So they make this place look like that and function like that even without gravity."

"Now you're a genius," said Sergeant, "but you didn't think of it till Carlotta . . ."

Sergeant's voice faded as Carlotta moved to stand between him and Ender, glaring into Sergeant's face.

"Mags zero," said Sergeant. In a moment he was flying gently up to the nearest cocoon. With his laser pistol he deftly severed the stem, then floated back down holding the cocoon by that half of the stem.

Ender shrank an expandable bag around the cocoon and put it into the sample pack. "Thanks," he said.

"Now you'll try to baby that thing to keep from damaging it," said Sergeant. "Which means you won't be much help fighting."

"Sergeant," said Carlotta, "he learned a lot from the exploded rab corpse you brought back in the Puppy; he can learn from the DNA in a crushed cocoon. So he's not going to baby it, he's going to do his job."

"He *was* going to baby it," said Sergeant, "until you said that."

Ender slapped his sample pack. Hard. "Eh," he said. "Andrew Delphiki, reporting for duty, sir."

Sergeant couldn't help smiling. "Point taken. All right, Carlotta, where do you want to go?"

"The thing I'm afraid of," said Carlotta, "is going out the wrong door and letting in a bunch of feral rabs. They'd go for the new slugs and make hash of the working rabs if they tried to interfere."

"If we sedated them, then when they collide with this bacterial soup, I think they'll stick," said Ender. "If they don't drown, they'll dissolve."

"We'll do as little damage as possible," said Sergeant, "but there's no point in leaving the way we came, because the tracks just loop back to the starting point."

Carlotta agreed, but still had no advice about where to go. "The question is, will the helm be located at the hub, where it's equally distant from all the rockets and sensors, so all the controls and connections are the same length? Or at one edge, where it might have viewports?"

"If it has viewports," said Sergeant, "then they'll be as far forward as possible, so that they get maximum protection from the rock."

"But what good are viewports that only look in one direction?" asked Carlotta. "This ship has circular symmetry, there's no belly or back, like our ships have."

"So the helm has viewports on every side?" asked Ender.

"Even at the narrowest point, just under the rock, the diameter is nearly nine hundred meters," said Sergeant. "That's a pretty big control room."

"So we forget about the viewports?" asked Ender.

"No," said Carlotta. "The five pillars absolutely duplicate each other. Redundancy. I think there are five control rooms, and they all have controls leading to every engine, and they all have viewports, so that if external sensors fail, they can still see."

Sergeant nodded. "And the control rooms are sealed off from each other, so damage to one doesn't cause atmosphere loss in the others."

"The pilots may be hiding from the feral rabs in just one of the control rooms," said Ender.

"So we go all the way forward," said Sergeant, "and then try for control rooms at the perimeter, exactly centered between the standpipes."

"Best view," said Carlotta.

"If the Formic workers ate these slugs, too," said Sergeant, "would there be a delivery system leading there?"

"I don't think so," said Ender. "The Hive Queen stays with the eggs and food comes to her. But the workers catch their meals between shifts."

"So it's all corridors, no tram tracks," said Carlotta.

"The question is, how far forward are we already?" asked Sergeant.

Good question. They had come a long way through the tram tunnel. "Map," said Carlotta.

A three-dimensional model of the ship seemed to stand half a meter away, in front of her visor. Of course there was nothing there at all—it was just an illusion on the visor itself. The visor could see where she looked and when she made a little popping sound with her lips, it zoomed in. A click with her tongue zoomed out.

"We're actually farther forward than the back of the rock," she said. "The Hive Queen is surrounded by rock above and at the sides. Anything with viewports is going to be aft of here."

"So we passed the helm getting here," said Sergeant, sounding frustrated.

"It's good to know what we learned here," said Carlotta. "Hive Queen dead, the function of the rabs, all this."

"And we were in a tunnel," said Ender. "We can only go where the tunnels lead us."

Sergeant made no answer, just led the way to one of the five obvious doors at the perimeter.

"How did you pick this one?" asked Carlotta.

"Eeny meeny," said Sergeant.

At the door, they found the cloud of debris again and a couple of eager rabs. A shot of gas and Carlotta closed the door again. At the next door, it was the same, and this time Sergeant led them through, they closed the door behind them, and fogged their way through to a passage leading aft—down, the way the corridors were oriented for Formics; to the right, the way they were oriented as they walked along the wall of the low wide tunnel so they could stand upright.

The passage was all afloat with the debris of feral rab life. "What are they finding to eat?" asked Carlotta.

"All the debris is rab body parts," said Ender. "They eat each other."

"Something has to be bringing nutrients into the system," said Sergeant contemptuously.

"Somebody's raiding the pantry," said Ender. "There were five ramps leading from the Queen's dais to five tram station doors. But the only one with active slugs was the one we came in on. But that doesn't mean the system isn't delivering slugs to all five trams. The feral rabs might be eating four-fifths of the food supply at the beginning of the tramways."

"What do you bet the slugs come from the ecotat?" said Carlotta. "That's where collection begins. But the slugs don't leave skeletal parts to float in the tunnels."

"All will be clear eventually," said Sergeant, "but for now let's keep our minds on task."

They were at a level now that Carlotta's map said should be just aft of the intersection of rock and hull. "If there are viewports at all, they could begin at this level."

"Maximum shelter," said Sergeant. "Let's give this level a shot."

They fogged the corridor and began to make the circuit. There were doors but they all led inward, toward the hub.

"Maybe we were wrong and the control room is in the hub," said Carlotta.

"Might as well see," said Sergeant.

They took up their standard positions at the door and Carlotta opened it.

It felt as if all the rabs on the ship leapt at her. Carlotta was knocked into the opposite wall. Both Sergeant and Ender sprayed like crazy, but it took several seconds for the rabs to fall into a stupor, and in that time, two got claws up under Carlotta's visor. If they had understood human anatomy, they could have severed her carotid artery, but instead they went for the soft place under her jaw. The pain was exquisite.

Carlotta tried to crawl away, but something had hold of her leg and wouldn't let go.

Sergeant. It was Sergeant holding her. All the rabs that had poured out of the inner chamber were inert, floating and bouncing around with the force of their original launch. Ender was still spraying fog into the room. Nothing was coming out.

"Bloody mess," muttered Sergeant. "Who ever knew the girl had so much blood in her?"

Paraphrasing *Macbeth*. He was trying to distract her. Or cope with his own fear. She reached up to remove her helmet but he already had it off. She was vaguely aware that he had yanked it past her ears despite a bit of snagging. It would have hurt if her jaw weren't being pounded with a hammer.

Within a minute, he had a coagulant pad in place and anesthetic was doing its job.

"Can you still use your tongue?" asked Sergeant. "Talk?"

Carlotta made a try. The anesthetic was numbing her tongue a little, but she could move it. "Talk fine," she said.

"Mumbling but good enough; you're still wired up right."

"Fast rab bastards," Carlotta said. Or meant to say. Tried to say.

"Funny," said Sergeant. So he had understood her. Or at least understood her intent.

"Mission aborted?" she asked.

"Are you insane?" asked Sergeant. "Let's see how you are in a minute when the meds have done a bit more work on you. Where's your stupid brother?"

She wanted to say, Right here, but there was no point in insulting him when he was tending to her wounds.

Ender came back then. "How's she doing?"

"Just soft flesh damage under the jaw. Nothing to the throat, and the meds will have it all healed up in a couple of hours."

"Wish I knew how long the sedatives would hold," said Ender.

"What were you doing in there?" asked Sergeant.

That's when Carlotta realized Ender must have gone inside the chamber that the rabs had come out of.

"They've made it their breeding chamber. They were protecting their young."

"Any queens?" asked Sergeant.

"More like seals—mothers and their pups gathered around them. Huge room."

"What was the room built for?" Carlotta asked. It sounded something like "Wha-roo-foe?" but apparently that was enough for her genius brothers.

"I think it's the control center," said Ender. "All the cabling is routed through there. Ductwork everywhere, ducts filled with cables and wires, lots of maintenance doors on everything."

"Rabs bothering any of it?" asked Sergeant.

"None of the doors was open," said Ender. "I closed the ones I opened. The rabs aren't smart enough to open maintenance doors."

"Maybe they were bred not to be door openers," said Sergeant.

"They certainly knew to gather at our door," said Ender.

"Heard us coming," said Carlotta.

"Probably," agreed Sergeant. "Attacking the puppies and mommies. We had to be dealt with."

"Safe to say the pilot's not in there," said Ender.

"And it wasn't the helm?" asked Sergeant.

Ender didn't even bother to answer.

Carlotta thought: What, you think the rabs bumped into the controls and got it into geosync by chance?

But then she thought: What if there was an automatic routine in the machinery, so that tripping a control had that effect? For that matter, what if there was no pilot at all, just an automatic orbit program?

No computers. The Hive Queens had no computers. All biological and mechanical and electrical, but not electronic. When Hive Queens wanted something to work automatically, they created a life-form to do it.

Her head had cleared. She was no longer in shock. It had been fifteen minutes. She could feel that the damage to her skin and salivary glands was healing. She reached for her helmet.

Sergeant reached out to restrain her, but only for a moment. "You sure?" he asked.

"Eh," she said. Then the helmet was on, and she was getting a report from it on the progress of her healing.

"Good fast work, Sergeant," said the Giant. "Ender, good recon. Carlotta, you're tough as nails."

"I wish," she said.

"Let's go before they wake up," said Sergeant. "I think this might still be the level of the helm or helms. If all the controls are routed through the hub, they must be coming from somewhere and leading to somewhere. Might be on this level."

But it wasn't. It was on the next level aft, which they reached an hour later. They also learned that the recovery time from the sedative mix was longer than that hour, because no rabs woke up. For all they knew, the fog was lethal and they'd never wake up.

Carlotta knew the door of a helm room when she saw it. It lay in the floor beneath their feet, and it was exceptionally wide and high. There was also a window in the door, and there was light on the other side. Bright light. Sunlight. They were on the side of the ship facing the sun right now.

"This isn't it," she said. "There has to be a way to block the sunlight when it's shining in the ports, and it isn't being blocked. But it'll be a room like this, farther along."

It took a while to work their way around the ship. They fogged the corridors as they went, because there was debris— but a lot less. And then Carlotta realized something and made them stop. "This sedative is going to work against the pilots, too—they're bound to be biologically related to Formics, even if they aren't Formics themselves. We've got to wait for the fog to dissipate before we open a door."

"The ventilation system is slow," said Ender.

"Maybe we want them to get a little dose of the sedative," said Sergeant. "Not a full spray, but whatever seeps in from the corridor."

"They won't like it," said Carlotta.

"If they're asleep, they won't mind anything," said Sergeant.

"Give us a chance to look at them without them looking at us," added Ender.

"And without them making the ship take off out of orbit so the Giant has to track us down," said Sergeant.

Carlotta conceded the point, though she still didn't like it. They opened the next helm door, a fifth of the way around the ship, where the sunlight wasn't so direct. It was a helm all right, several Formic-shaped perches and control sets. Lots of unlabeled dials and displays that consisted of arrangements of small lights. And perches in front of the viewports, so observers could be stationed there.

But there wasn't a soul in the room. Not even a corpse.

"Proof of concept, anyway," said Sergeant. "Now we know that helm rooms are arranged symmetrically around the hull, and not hidden away in the hub."

"And we know the Formics wanted to look, not just take the Hive Queen's data," said Ender.

"Or this is how she got her data," said Carlotta.

"Could be," said Sergeant. "Observers in all the helm rooms, but actual pilots in only one."

"So let's go find the one," she said.

Sergeant seemed not to mind that she had, in effect, pre-emptively given the order. He led the way back into the corridor. No need for more spray—the fog they had originally sprayed was still spreading through this corridor all the way around the ship. In smaller concentration, it wasn't so quick—there were rabs still waggling their limbs and jaws. But Sergeant and Ender didn't spray again. These rabs weren't trying to attack anything, they were trying to stay awake. And failing.

The third helm was dark. Nightside. But when Carlotta shone her helmlight on the door, she pointed to shininess on the metal near the lower and upper sills. This door had been opened repeatedly in recent years.

They got in position. Carlotta stood away from where the opening would be—lesson learned—and shifted the lever. The door slid open.

Nothing came out. Not a sound from inside.

Sergeant lowered himself into the room and drifted downward, toward the wall with the viewports, setting his helmet to illuminate the room and do a sweep of motion search.

"No movement," he said softly. "But there's a heat source."

Carlotta came into the room.

Ender hesitated at the doorway. "Keep watch out here?" he asked.

"Come in and shut the door," said Sergeant. "We may have found our pilots."

Carlotta got to the windowed wall and then followed Sergeant as he walked lightly toward the control bay of the helm.

Unmoving, several small shapes with iridescent colors clung to the control panel. They were smaller than Carlotta, about half her height, but longer than the rabs. They had wings—that was the iridescence. No claws. In fact, the two front arms on each side seemed to be fused together, parting only near the end. But the "Y" formed by the ends of the feet was able to grasp levers and controls. And the jaws were Formic-like, also able to grasp.

The eyes were not placed normally. They were on the top of the head, not quite on stalks, but not embedded in the skull, either. They moved and tracked all three children as they approached.

"What are they?" asked Carlotta softly. "Did the Hive Queens breed special pilot creatures?"

"I don't think so," said Ender softly. "Look at how thin they are. And weak looking. And the way the hind legs have hooks. And those eyes on the tops of their heads. They weren't designed for piloting."

"What, then?" asked Sergeant.

"They weren't designed at all," said Ender. "Except by evolution."

"How do you know that?"

"Because they're built to attach themselves to something.

Those rear hooks—not for walking. And the wings look like they work. They fly—that's why they're so thin."

"Big heads, though," said Carlotta.

"Smart?" asked Sergeant.

"Smartish," said Ender. "Smart enough to put a ship into orbit."

"Smart enough to understand what we're saying?" asked Sergeant.

"Maybe if they had ears," said Ender. "But Formics don't have any organs for hearing, just sensing vibrations. They know we're making noises but they don't know why."

"Formics?" asked Sergeant. "These are Formics?"

"Pretty sure," said Ender.

"Why didn't they die when the Hive Queen died?" asked Carlotta.

"Very interesting question," said Ender. "But maybe they don't react the way the workers do. Maybe when a Hive Queen dies, they stay alive so they can attach to the next one."

"Attach?" asked Carlotta. "A parasite?"

"A useful one," said Ender. "I think these are the Formic males. They spend their lives attached to the Hive Queen. So she can draw on their genes whenever she needs to."

"But she was so big," said Carlotta.

"Sexual dimorphism," said Sergeant.

"Wait," said Ender. "I think we're as close as they can bear. That one is about to take flight."

Carlotta could see it now, too. The wings were extending.

The eyes were standing straight up. "Is there any hope of communicating with them?" she asked.

"I hope we're communicating lack of threat," said Ender. "Don't point your hands at them. Set the shotguns down."

"No," said Sergeant.

"You're right," said Ender. "But the two of you back away, all right? Let me go in unarmed and alone."

Carlotta immediately complied; a moment later, Sergeant reached the same conclusion. Ender sent his shotgun drifting slowly toward Sergeant. He took off his helmet and sent it toward Carlotta. Then he rolled over onto his back.

Carlotta realized that this put his eyes on the top of his head, like the Formic eyes. She caught his helmet and held it.

Ender was keeping his arms down at his sides as he drifted toward the control panel where the Formics waited. Carlotta realized he was treating his arms like wings, showing them folded against his body. He was imitating their posture. Was this how the Formics showed submission? Were they submitting to us, and is Ender now submitting to them?

As Ender drifted closer to them, the Formics began to move. They were so small. Staying hooked to various controls—controls that were definitely not designed for their use, Carlotta could see that now—three of the five of them reached out for Ender's head.

She heard Sergeant's quick intake of breath.

"Let him be," came the Giant's voice softly through the helmets. "It's a chance that he has to take."

Carlotta could not help but marvel at Ender's stillness as the Formic males reached out and touched his head, bringing him carefully to a stop. Those Y-shaped claws, the mouths so near his face. The residual pain in her jaw reminded her of how dangerous it could be to let aliens near your head.

The three formics who were holding him lowered their mouths toward his head. The other two were standing watch, it seemed.

They pressed the tips of their forejaws against Ender's head.

Ender let out a low moan, almost a cry.

Sergeant started forward.

"No," said the Giant.

Carlotta caught Sergeant, helped him back down to where his boots could remagnetize to the floor.

Ender sighed again. Again. Then his voice came, an urgent whisper. "Don't hurt them," he said. "They're showing me."

"Showing you what?" asked Carlotta, trying to keep her voice soft, to keep the fear out of it. Who knew what sense the Formics could make of the sounds they managed to hear?

"Everything," said Ender. "How they've lived since the Queen died."

CHAPTER 9

Drones and Workers

Ender had never felt such loss of control over his own mind. Even in a nightmare, when nothing is going the way you want, the images still came from somewhere. You knew what you were seeing.

But the images that started passing through his mind the moment the Formic males touched him were chaotic and strange. Half the time he didn't even know what he was seeing.

Slow down! He felt as if his mind were shouting at them. Yet they did not respond at all. He caught glimpses of this and that. The Hive Queen alive. The small males flying around her, and then landing on her. Some she batted away, but others she helped stay in place while they attached. Images of the Hive Queen's own hand bringing slugs to the mouths of the males.

But as Ender experienced it, the slugs came to his own mouth. He smelled them, he saw them wriggle, and they looked delicious. His mouth watered. He was so, so hungry.

As soon as something made a little sense, though, the image changed. Did they know he had understood and so they moved on? If they could tell he understood them, why couldn't they hear his plea that they slow down?

Because you're framing it in words, idiot.

Ender tried to picture someone moving slowly, but their images overwhelmed what he was imagining. Then, desperate for communication, he tried simply *feeling* sluggish. Heavy-lidded. Tired.

He got a jolt of some strong emotion that would certainly have wakened him, if he had really been dozing off. The emotion wasn't anger, it was—alertness. They sent him what they wanted him to feel.

They were definitely in control of this exchange.

He tried something else. He took an image they gave him— this time it seemed to be rabs bouncing around in a corridor— and tried to freeze it. Hold still. Wait.

Immediately they sent the image again; again he froze it. Examined it.

And now they understood. The next image came, not as a pure memory, in motion, but rather as a frozen moment.

It's not that they don't have language, thought Ender. They can blurt, they can be too excited, they can slow down and speak methodically. The images are not random. I'm not getting a complete memory dump. They send images, but also desires, responses. And they notice what I'm doing in my own mind and respond to that.

For all he knew this kind of communication had a grammar to it, and he was speaking with the equivalent of a foreign accent. It didn't matter, as long as they spoke to him slowly.

Now he saw the image of a Hive Queen, tall, magnificent; he felt the devotion they felt for her, and the hunger as well. They needed to be close to her.

She was covered with drones. If Ender hadn't seen her without the males, he would have assumed their backs *were* her belly, they coated her so completely.

Then he felt himself become one of the drones. Again the image of her feeding him, but as she lowered the slug toward his mouth, she let go of it. The slug dropped away out of reach.

The world seemed to sway; it was the Queen swaying. Then she lay down, half coiling within the circle of her private zone. Even as she pulled herself downward, she made sure not to crush any of her males. She was protecting them, loving them till the end.

Then Ender felt something vital go out of his mind. He realized that the warmth and light he had felt when he was one of the attached drones was the mind of the Hive Queen. And now it was gone.

The males, one by one, detached. As one of them, Ender understood that it was time for them to look for a new queen.

She hadn't eaten them, so they were valued highly and allowed to help a new queen seed the hive.

They rose into the air and flew. Around them was the constant pushing and shepherding of the slugs, the rabs, coming up all the ramps.

Something else, though. Formic workers, becoming limp. Unlike the Queen, they didn't pull themselves down to the ground. They drifted, floated, rose, fell, depending on the eddies of air in the Hive Queen's chamber.

All these images of dying Formics came as still pictures, one after another—it was a change from when he *was* an attached drone, then a flying one.

There was no Queen. Nothing but Formic workers, and they were all dying. All dead.

The drones circled, explored. Ender realized that all of them were conveying images to each other. It made a cacophony of pictures, almost impossible to understand. But they were skilled at sorting through it all.

Now Ender understood that the chaos he had felt before was each of the drones putting his own version of their message and their memories into Ender's mind at the same time. He hadn't the strength of consciousness to push any of them out of the way himself. So when they seemed to slow things down, Ender now realized that they had simply designated one of them to speak for all. Now a single drone was putting images into his mind. But since he had experienced the desperate search for a new queen, each drone pressing images into the minds of the others, that was now what he gave to Ender.

Again Ender tried to freeze the image, but instead the drone moved on. He felt a sense of loss, emptiness. It wasn't just the death of the Queen. The drones had images of every part of the ship, many of which Ender recognized from his travels. But each view ended abruptly; he was momentarily blind.

He realized what they were saying in this image-language. The drones had shared in the Queen's connection with all the Formic workers. They were the minds most closely bound with hers, and she shared everything with them.

They understood the whole ship. They were used to being able to watch any part of the ship at any time. When she died, they might have continued to connect with the Formic workers. But they died with the Queen. All that remained to the drones was each other's vision, and since they were all in the same room, they were all seeing the same thing. Dead Queen. Rabs herding the slugs up the ramps. Dead Formic workers.

They went to a door. They had never opened one with their own limbs. But they all had the memory of being inside the mind of a worker when she opened the door. They knew exactly where the lever was and how it felt to work it. Only it was hard. The drone's hand slipped off the lever twice—and to Ender, as if in a nightmare, it felt as if his own hand had slipped off.

But the door opened eventually and they flew outside. One of them stopped to close the door. Ender *was* that one for a moment; then he was a different one.

They all had the same destination: the helm. Ender knew

what the place felt like to the drones. It was the most vital work of the whole colony. No matter what the Queen had been doing at any given moment, one or another of the drones always looked out through the eyes of the worker who was sitting at the helm, watching her choices, her actions. The guidance of the ship, the health of the ship, always there was a drone involved.

Then a realization swept over Ender and made him shudder. Just as the drones each had their own mind, separate from the Queen's, no matter how tightly they were linked, so also the Formic at the controls had had her own mind, her own will. *She was piloting the ship.* The Hive Queen had given an order—an image of what was wanted—but the worker was carrying out the labor herself. The worker understood the task. The drones didn't control her; they sat inside her mind and observed, prompting her now and then, but *she* was doing it.

The Formic workers were not just extensions of the Queen's mind. The strength of her mind overwhelmed them; they had no choice but to obey. And when the Hive Queen wasn't paying direct attention to the Formic pilot, one or more of the drones was watching.

Why? Because the Hive Queen wanted them to.

And why did she want them to? What had she feared might happen if they did not?

Ender had no way to frame the question. He could only guess. If the Formic workers had minds of their own, perhaps there were occasional individuals who could resist the power of the Queen's mind. Perhaps there were free workers.

Thinking of free workers made him realize that the workers who obeyed the Hive Queen as perfectly as they could, they were slaves. They were her daughters, but she refused to let them have minds of their own.

Yet the worker had piloted a starship. It hadn't understood the astrophysics, the mathematics, but it understood the Hive Queen's plans and orders, and it carried them out using its own mind, its own skills and habits and experience.

We misunderstood them completely, thought Ender. We thought the Hive Queen *was* the mind of the whole colony. But she was not. They had their own wills, just like humans, but she had the power to force obedience. And when *she* wasn't checking on them, the drones were.

The drones, too, had minds of their own, more powerful than the Formic workers' minds. They had an intensity of mental connection that even the Hive Queen didn't have.

How did Ender know that? Because the drones knew it, were proud of it. Because as they watched him think of these things, they interpreted them and responded to them.

For Ender was no longer trying to shout words at them within his mind. Now he was realizing things without words, or with mere fragments of sentences that did not stand alone; images, feelings swept through his mind and he wondered, Is this how we all think? The deep mind, the mind that is older than language—the mind of the same kind as the Hive Queen's mind—humans had one. Language was an overlay, so loud that it usually shouted out all the other thoughts in the human mind.

Whenever I think about thinking, my thoughts become words. It is the language talking at me. But the language came from outside. I think I control it, but it controls me back. Like the Hive Queen in the minds of the drones, language becomes part of the background noise, the air I breathe, gravity; it's just there.

Until it's gone.

Language acts in the human mind the way the Hive Queen acts in the minds of the other Formics. It shapes us without our understanding how we're being shaped. When the Hive Queen put a desire into a Formic worker's mind, the worker felt it as her own desire. Just so did the thousand voices of language give shape to Ender's thoughts, without his really being aware of how the language was shaping him. Only when the language fell silent and then returned did he become aware of what it was doing when it returned.

But there was nothing subtle about the Hive Queen's control of her worker-daughters. She was overwhelming. They were swallowed up. And even when only the drones remained in a worker's mind, watching, they overwhelmed the worker. In some ways, because their whole attention was devoted to the immediate task, the drones had a stronger presence in the workers' minds.

When the workers died, the drones were left to themselves, to each other. They had lost the Queen. Unlike the workers, they experienced her, not as a suffocating force, but rather as a being of light, an angel in their minds. She loved them and they never forgot it for an instant. But besides losing the Queen, they had also lost the workers. They had lost their vision of the whole ship.

That's why they went to the helm. It was the most important job of all. They could no longer see what was happening. But they *had* to see, and since there was no daughter queen to attach to, to restore the network of vision, the drones went to the helm themselves.

Once they got there—here, Ender realized—they pulled the workers' bodies off their perches and set them adrift. The drones remembered all the tasks that the workers had done while the drones were inside their minds; now they carried out those tasks. Checking the instruments. Looking through the viewports.

They kept watching. Monitoring. Because it was the job that must be done. They didn't wonder whether there was any point in doing it, without a queen to repopulate the ship with workers. They did what had to be done, as long as it was within their ability.

At first they even tried to do maintenance, but that job was quickly abandoned. For the rabs assigned to cleanup work were going feral. Their job was to eat anything spilled or dead in the corridors. When the Queen and all the workers died, they had an enormous feast of dead Formics throughout the ship. It was their job. The drones even let them into the helm to take apart and consume the bodies of the Formics.

With the overabundance of food, the rab population grew;

then all the dead Formics they could find were eaten, and the rabs were still there.

They had a job hardwired in their genes: to shepherd, and to scavenge. They were also trained to defecate only in the ecotat—or outdoors in nature, as they thought of it. When the last dead Formics were consumed, they found that their population had expanded too fast. There wasn't enough to eat. They were starving.

The Hive Queen would never have allowed such a thing— her mind, when it turned toward the rabs, had so much power that she could kill excess rabs just by noticing them.

But the drones, while they could easily see inside the rab mind, hadn't the destructive power of a Hive Queen. And the rabs were too stupid for the drones to control them. They couldn't receive and remember an order.

So the rabs went wild. Or rather, a few of them went wild, but within a few generations, those wild ones were the only ones still reproducing in the corridors of the ship.

The drones realized what was happening in time to seal off the Hive Queen's chamber and their own helm. They also sealed off the doors leading "outside," or into the ecotat.

This drove the rabs insane. Cut off not only from a supply of corpses but also from any access to the slugs, they went crazy, eating each other, eating their mates, their own young.

But in their frenzy they broke into four of the tram tubes. Now the rabs inside the ecotat, as they collected slugs and put them into the trams, were really feeding the feral rabs. Only one tram continued to send unneeded slugs into the Queen's lair. The only reason the rabs left that one alone was that they were getting plenty to eat from the other four. It didn't occur to their tiny minds to search for more.

All of this Ender received through visions and feelings put into his mind. It was a constant struggle to make sense of what he was seeing, but he never lost track of the intensity of purpose that the drones felt as they, through the one drone, "talked" to him.

They knew who he was. Or rather, they knew who humans were. They well remembered the Hive Queen's grief when she experienced the loss of all the other Hive Queens when the human fleet erased the Formic home world centuries ago. Whether this meant that these very drones had been alive at the time, or they merely experienced the Hive Queen's vivid memories of the tragedy, Ender could not tell. Maybe the drones themselves didn't know.

What mattered was that the drones urgently needed something from the humans who had come to their ship.

It finally dawned on him what they wanted. Give us the Hive Queen.

What Hive Queen? He framed the question by thinking of a queen and then having an urgent questioning attitude. It didn't work—it was really the same message they were sending him. Where is she?

He tried something else. He pictured each of his sibs and himself, and showed that they were also searching for the

Hive Queen. He showed them searching through the *Herodotus* and finding nothing. He hoped they were getting the message: We have no Hive Queen.

In reply, an image came into his mind, a very clear one. A young man under the open sky of a planet, carrying a cocoon like the one Ender had in his sample case.

"They want a cocoon," said Ender. "Get the cocoon we took and give it to them."

The drones let go of him and his mind came back. No, his mind had been there all along. He had simply lost full control of it until the drones left him alone. He felt so small and empty. He had never truly felt like a child before, since his life was built around children the same size, and the Giant, who bore no comparison. Now Ender felt how lonely it was to be locked into your own mind, with only the bossiness of language to keep him company.

Ender opened his eyes and maneuvered himself to watch as Carlotta opened the sample case and took out the cocoon.

At once the drones swarmed to it, seized it, flew with it to the middle of the room, pressed themselves against it.

After a long moment, they let go of it and flew together to a corner of the room, where they swarmed, but not in the normal way. They kept bumping into each other—hard enough that it would bruise a human. Bumping, bumping.

And he realized: They're grieving. They're so sad.

The cocoon continued drifting. Ender moved near it, caught it, returned it to the sample case.

As soon as the case was closed, a drone came back to him,

flying so fast that Ender thought he was being attacked. He caught a glimpse of the ever-alert Sergeant aiming the fog at the drone, but Ender didn't even have to say no. Carlotta put out a restraining hand.

The drone landed and latched on to him. Images flooded Ender's mind again, but not in the confused way. There was despair and hunger in the drone's message, but he was not angry. Nor were the other drones, whom Ender could sense contributing to the message. The cocoon that Ender had offered them was empty. Dead. It was just another of the cocoons from the Queen's chamber—they had all died with the Queen.

But they knew of a living Queen, one who had never been on this ship. They needed her now. A human had her, and they could even show Ender his face, but he had no idea who it was.

They showed him the inside of the ecotat, all the plants, the small animals. Trees, insects, grasses, flowers, roots, small climbers, creepers, all inside the cylinder.

They showed him Formic workers loading plants and animals into the huge insectile landing vehicles and launching them down through the atmosphere, where they opened and Formic workers unloaded them, planted things, reducing all the native flora and fauna to protoplasmic goo like the vile liquid in the Hive Queen's lair.

It's what they were doing on Earth during the scouring of China. Turn the native life-forms into a nutrient-rich soup and then start growing useful Formic plants and animals in it.

But as soon as it was clear that Ender understood, the drone pointedly made the Formic workers disappear.

Then another image of the Formic landing vehicle opening up. Instead of a Formic worker coming out, this time it was a drone. But it wasn't flying. It was creeping on the surface. It was being crushed by the gravity of the planet. It was dying.

They need a Hive Queen. They can't live on a planet's surface unless they're clinging to a queen.

They showed him again the young man with the cocoon, only this time they showed the cocoon opening up under a bright sun on a planet full of life, and when the cocoon tore open, what came out was a Hive Queen.

Ender blotted out that image. I don't have a Hive-Queen-in-a-cocoon for you. Instead he tried to show them images of himself and Sergeant and Carlotta unloading things, planting things. But the drone who was touching him rejected the image, blotting it out. It replaced the image with a picture of hundreds of Formic workers swarming over the surface of the world, tending fields, carrying loads, building things—and then he erased the workers.

For some reason they couldn't accept the idea of humans planting their flora and fauna on the planet.

No, no, Ender was missing the point, thinking like a human. They were showing him that the whole thing was pointless to them if there was no queen to populate the world.

Ender was getting more adept with the image-language,

and now he repeated back to them the image of the dying Formic workers at the time of the Hive Queen's death. Why? He pushed his inquiry at them with great urgency. Why did the Formic workers die?

They answered him by showing the dead Hive Queen.

Why does the death of the Hive Queen cause the death of the workers?

He had no idea if they really understood. They simply showed the dead Hive Queen again.

So Ender tried juxtaposition. He remembered the dead Hive Queen, then the dying Formics, but then contrasted them with the swarming drones. Dying workers, living drones, dying workers, living drones, and all the time his urgent inquiry.

The drones watched these images, his inquiry, till he had repeated them several times.

Then the messenger let go of him and retreated to the distant corner where the others awaited him.

"What did you say?" asked Sergeant. "Did you piss them off?"

"They know this cocoon is dead," said Ender, "and they want a live one."

"Well, abracadabra," said Carlotta. "What do they think we are? Wizards?"

"They think there's a living Hive Queen in a cocoon somewhere. A human has her. I saw him—they know his face, it's the same face every time. When they saw our ship and realized we were human, they thought we were bringing that cocoon with us. They thought that's what I had in the sample case."

"Sorry to be such a disappointment," said Sergeant. "Why would they think a Hive Queen cocoon survived?"

Then the two who were wearing their helmets grew quiet, listening. "The Giant's laughing," said Carlotta.

"Put your helmet on," said Sergeant. "You want to hear this."

"My helmet tells them I'm done talking with them, and I'm not."

Sergeant sighed, but Carlotta came close to Ender, sat beside him. He could hear the Giant faintly now.

"It's the Speaker for the Dead," the Giant said. "The Speaker for the Dead has that cocoon. She's alive inside it, that Hive Queen. That's why he could interview her and write his book."

So *The Hive Queen* was based on truth after all. And these Formics knew about it because all Hive Queens were in constant contact with each other.

But not the drones. Ender realized that the moment the Hive Queen died, the drones had contact only with each other. Their mental powers were much greater than those of the workers, but they didn't match the Hive Queen's ability to project her mental control or contact over seemingly infinite distances. The drones had to be close.

The messenger drone returned and landed on his head.

It had a different message now. Ender saw the life of these

drones for the past century. There had been twenty. Now there were only five.

Ender saw the death of each one. It was numbingly alike. They opened the door, and while most of the drones fought off the attacking rabs, a few would fly past them, outmaneuvering the rabs. They went to the ecotat and entered through a portal known only to them. The feral rabs could not get through it.

Inside the ecotat, they would gather all the slugs they could and then fly back, slowly, burdened with the clinging slugs.

As they neared the helm, they would pry off a slug or two and fling it near the horde of rabs pressing against the door of the helm. The rabs immediately went into a feeding frenzy. While they were distracted, the door opened again, and the drones flew in with their remaining slugs.

Only now and then a rab noticed them and bounded upward, clawing. One by one over the centuries, drones were killed. And as fewer drones remained, it became harder to fight off the rabs at the door, and more dangerous.

The expeditions to the ecotat ended. Instead, they opened the door just a crack and closed it at once. Then they fought the rabs that got in, killed them, peeled them, ate them.

But their flesh was nauseating to eat, and worse, they lost more of their brother drones in fighting the rabs that got in. It had been a long time since they had dared to do any such thing. They had been fasting. Two of the drones had died of starvation. The others ate their bodies—not a strange thing to do, in Formic terms, for the Queen herself would eat drones that she no longer found useful, then cause an egg to hatch as a drone and bring it to take the eaten one's place. Drones were, in a word, delicious.

That's what had kept these five alive till now.

Ender reached into his sample case himself and took out the two slugs he had collected. They were still very much alive; Ender had a clear enough memory of the images of the drones feasting on slugs that he now thought of them as delicious, though of course humans could not metabolize half the proteins in their squirmy bodies.

The drone that had been talking to him waited till last, allowing the others to feed first. The drones were small enough that Ender could see that even a portion of a slug was a substantial meal.

They saved a good part of both slugs for the drone-who-talked-to-humans. He ate last; he ate best.

While they ate, Ender summarized what he had learned.

"I think that meal saved their lives," said Ender.

"A little hard on the slugs," said Sergeant.

"I think they would have been better with cinnamon," said Carlotta.

Ender ignored their humor. There was no such thing as Formic humor, and he was feeling very Formic right now. "They don't see any point in seeding this planet if they don't have a Hive Queen. And we have none to give them."

"At least we can get them food," said Sergeant. "And tame these feral rabs. In fact, we can kill them, if they want. The ship is theirs, so the rabs are theirs, and if they want them dead, we can sedate them and then blast them all. Make the ship safe for the drones again."

"I'll offer," said Ender. "But it won't change the pointlessness of their lives."

"Won't change the pointlessness of ours, either," said Sergeant.

CHAPTER 10

The Giant Moves

The whole time they were in the ark, it was all Bean could do to keep silent. He had commanded so many times in the field that it almost killed him to be a silent observer. The problem was that almost everything he thought of doing, so did Cincinnatus or one of the other children.

The helmets fed their data into one of the computers on *Herodotus* and constructed a three-dimensional model of their movements in the holodisplay of Bean's primary computer. The picture was never complete—whatever the helmets hadn't observed was left blank. But their movements began to construct a map of the ark. All very useful.

When the rabs in their breeding chamber swarmed over the children and he saw two of them get claws up under Carlotta's visor, Bean almost died. His heart gave several mighty heaves in his chest and then was ominously still. A couple of alarms went off. Bean even felt the shooting pain in his left shoulder and arm that was a harbinger of the end.

But drugs were fed into his veins automatically, and his heart rate returned to normal.

Ironic, if the rabs killed me *just because I couldn't stop watching the children.*

He feared for them; he was proud of them. They, having known no one but each other and a giant for five of their six years, had no idea of how impossibly small they seemed. The words coming out of their mouths still astonished him. The depth of their analysis, their quickness of thought. *If I sounded like them on the streets of Rotterdam, no wonder Sister Carlotta rescued me. I did not belong there.*

As these children would be completely out of place in an American first grade, or biding their time in Finland till they turned seven. Carlotta could pass any engineering degree; Ender could get a doctorate, since much of his work would qualify for a dissertation if Bean had made him write it up properly. Cincinnatus could get into any military academy in the world and be top cadet, except for that little thing about age and size, and the fact that no adult would follow him.

Yet adults *had* followed children in the Third Formic War, the final one. Bean had been one of those children. He had sent men to their death, and unlike Ender he knew it.

But it's one thing to send adult soldiers, all of whom were volunteers, into battle with a high risk of death. To send six-year-olds, even brilliant ones, *especially* brilliant ones, the only hope of their new species—that was unconscionable.

Yet Bean had sent them, because he knew they had to test themselves. When Bean died they would bear full responsibility for a powerful starship and, if Bean had his way, for the Formic ark and a new planet as well. Now he knew they were ready.

What chilled him, though, were the things Ender reported about his conversation with the drones. How quickly he had learned to make himself understood to a people without language! The courage he had shown in letting them enter his mind. But then they told him things, impossible things. The Formic workers had minds of their own? The Hive Queens suppressed them?

This was not even hinted at in Ender Wiggin's book *The Hive Queen.* Either his son Ender had mistaken their meaning, or his friend Ender Wiggin had been lied to by the cocooned Hive Queen he was carrying around from world to world.

Ender, you poor man! How did they find you? How did they get the treasure of their species into your hands? And why did you take on the responsibility? *The Hive Queen* had changed the opinion of most people, so that now Ender Wiggin was called "Ender the Xenocide" and his victory had become known as an unspeakable war crime. All this Ender Wiggin bore—no, *caused*—in order to make amends with a people that he believed he had completely destroyed.

But when they encountered Ender Wiggin, when he wrote *The Hive Queen,* the Hive Queen he spoke to had known about this ark. The Hive Queen aboard the colony ship had not yet died. Yet Ender Wiggin was given to believe that the sole survivor of the Formic species was in his hands. How many other ancient colony ships like this were there? How many others had the Formics sent out during the years when the International Fleet was making its way to all their known colony worlds? For all Bean knew, the Formics already had a hundred worlds, and were merely biding their time.

One thing was certain: Bean had to talk to these drones himself. He had to *know* what they knew, for it seemed they knew everything that the Hive Queen knew.

Or perhaps not. Perhaps she only used them to help her monitor the ship, to help her control the workers. She might have kept any number of secrets from them. Why should she tell them everything? She communed with other Hive Queens that way, but with lesser beings, with tools, with slaves, why would she?

Still, he had to know, for himself, what the drones knew. Not that he didn't believe Ender's reporting—the boy simply lacked the context that Bean would bring to such a mental conversation.

The problem was that Bean could hardly expect the drones to come to him. Leave their ship? Their responsibility to the ship had kept them alive for a century after their Queen died.

Even now, they lived only in the hope of saving their ship by finding another queen. They wouldn't *leave* the ship—what could Bean offer them?

So if he was to find out the truth about the Hive Queens, he would have to go to them.

On the ship, the children obeyed the drones' request that they wipe out the feral rabs. There were plenty of domestic rabs alive in the ecotat and the Hive Queen's chamber. By finding and killing all the feral rabs, the children were rendering the drones' lives bearable. They could feed on slugs to their hearts' content. Their debt of gratitude to the humans— no, the antonines, the leguminotes—would be considerable.

If Formics could feel gratitude. Were the drones deceiving them, too?

It took the children a couple of hours to clear out the ship, with drones leading them to every pocket of feral rabs. By this, Bean learned something else: The drones' mental abilities extended to sensing the tiny minds of the rabs. What were the individual workers capable of, if the Hive Queen had ever let them alone? Did they have mental abilities comparable to the drones'? Could they "talk" to each other directly? Or would the Queen always sense the conversation and put a stop to it?

Why did they die when the Queen died? Why *didn't* the drones die? They were, if anything, *more* dependent on the Queen, and yet when she lay down and died they flew away. Only the workers died. Why?

So many questions.

"Mission accomplished," said Cincinnatus. "Permission to return to *Herodotus*."

Bean wanted to say, Yes, brilliantly done, come to my arms, my beamish boy! But he needed more information if he was to accomplish what he knew he had to do before he died. "How tired are you?" he asked. "It's been a long day."

Cincinnatus polled the others. "Tired, but . . . what do you have in mind?"

"Two things," said Bean. "Ender's samples—he needs to get a sample from the drones. Enough to run their genome and compare it to the genome from the dead cocoon. So we can compare male and female, drone and worker."

Ender spoke up. "You want to know why the drones didn't die."

"Maybe it was a disease that affected only females. But then, why did the workers not die until the Queen did, and then all at once?"

"They might have already been dying," said Ender. "That was outside the purview of what they were telling me."

"But the drones didn't die," said Bean.

"I'll try to negotiate a biopsy on some body part that contains their genome. Maybe they kept some relic of the dead ones."

"The ones they ate?"

"Different species, different rules," said Carlotta, almost reflexively.

"And you, Carlotta," said Bean.

"You shouldn't have spoken up," said Cincinnatus.

"I already had this planned," said Bean. "While Ender's getting his samples, Carlotta, I need you to figure out a way to get me into the ecotat."

The children were silent.

"No," said Carlotta.

"They must have built the ark with a plan for getting large quantities of plants and animals out of there to ship it down to the planet's surface. However they plan to get that stuff out, I can go in that way."

"It'll kill you," said Ender.

"You're going to dock the Hound with *Herodotus* at the cargo bay. With both doors open and gravity turned off, a six-year-old could push me into the Hound."

They were not amused by his "six-year-old" joke. "Father," said Cincinnatus, "you're too fragile. What can you do here that we can't do for you?"

"Bring my entire store of knowledge to bear in my conversation with the drones," said Bean honestly.

"Couldn't we bring them to you?"

"Don't even hint at the possibility," said Bean. "If you suggested taking them away from the ark, they might easily interpret it as an attempt by us to steal the ark from them. They may have asked you to do it, but they just saw you wield death to all the feral rabs. They also shared their Queen's memory of the deaths of all the other Hive Queens in the Third Formic War. Why wouldn't they assume we had death on our minds?"

"If you die on the way . . ." Carlotta began.

"I could have died a year ago. Or two. I'm glad for every minute I get, as long as I can watch you becoming what you're growing up to be."

"The Giant's getting sentimental," said Cincinnatus.

"Careful you don't drown in his big puddly tears," said Ender.

Old jokes, family customs. "You know what I want you to do. If I die in the process of trying to get more data for you, so be it. You'll do fine without it, or learn enough eventually to find it out yourself. But I might not die, and we should plan on that. You'll be glad to know what I learn, I think, if I live to learn it."

Another silence. On the holodisplay, Bean could see them take off their helmets. They thought that meant he couldn't hear them. The simple naïveté of children.

Their conversation was brief, but it consisted mostly of thinking up ways to get the Giant to change his mind.

When they put their helmets back on, Bean preempted them. "You have work to do," he said. "Carlotta, come back with a plan to get me into the ecotat, or don't come back. Ender, get a sample."

"What about me?" asked Cincinnatus.

"Stay with Ender and protect him. I don't think Carlotta will be in any danger."

"No sir," said Cincinnatus. "We stay together. We all watch while Ender gets his sample from the drones, if he can. Then we all go with Carlotta."

"It'll take more time. You're already tired."

"As you said, the ship is safe now. We can sleep here and start again tomorrow, if need be."

Cincinnatus was right. How could Bean say, I'm eager for you to get these things done and get back here, because I might not be alive tomorrow or the next day. His whole argument had been that he was *not* going to die.

"The Giant is thinking," said Cincinnatus.

"The vibrations pass through the vacuum of space and make me want to urinate," said Ender.

"Again," said Carlotta.

"I think it's a rule that it's socially acceptable to wet yourself when aliens enter your mind for the first time," said Ender. "If it wasn't already, it is now."

They were so immature. And so adult. The weight of a species on their shoulders. Children bantering on the playground, teasing their old crippled father.

"Do what you're going to do, and get back to me as soon as you've done it," said Bean.

"Say 'please,'" said Carlotta.

"Say 'yes sir,'" answered Bean.

A moment's pause.

"Yes sir," said Carlotta.

"That pleases me very much," said Bean.

"That doesn't count as 'please,'" said Carlotta.

"It's all the 'please' you're going to get." Bean could play at playground banter, too.

In the end, the drones solved both problems. When Ender asked them for samples, they all solemnly peeled off sections of skin. If it hurt them, they gave no sign. And then they led Carlotta to the cargo loading area.

It was a deft design. A second wheel, almost as large in diameter but far smaller in depth, was attached to the forward end of the great cylinder of the ecotat. It could lock to the ecotat, or it could break free, slow down, and stop relative to the rest of the ship. It was the movement equivalent of an airlock.

Around the edges, the trams entered the wheel from their five tracks that led to the Queen's chamber. Once the tram was entirely inside the wheel, the wheel would start to spin until it matched the rotation of the ecotat. Then doors opened into the ecotat, and the domestic rabs there would fill them with slugs. When they closed the door, the wheel desynchronized with the ecotat and rejoined the ship.

Cargo was a different matter. Above the tramways—closer to the hub than to ground level inside the ecotat—there were five huge doors, six meters square, which synched between the wheel and the ecotat. On the other side of the wheel, though, all five bays opened into a huge cargo chamber. Without spin, that space was weightless. So objects much longer than the depth of the wheel could be loaded into the bays surrounding the great doors.

The cargo bay, in turn, was accessible through two even larger airlocks. Carlotta had the helmets take minute measurements, and they concluded that the Hound could fit in the larger of the two airlocks. "We can bring the entire ship inside the cargo area, and then transfer you, weightless, through the cargo doors into the ecotat," Carlotta reported.

"So it's not so impossible," said Bean. "I might even live through it."

"No, you won't," said Carlotta. "The centrifugal force inside the ecotat gives too strong a gravitational effect. Three times what you're experiencing now. When you drift into the ecotat, you're fine—weightless. But then you have to get down to the ground. If we just drop you, you won't be going the same speed as the floor of the cylinder. There's an impact. That will kill you. Or you can climb down the ladders that the Formics use. That way they gradually acquire the rotation of the cylinder and reach the ground perfectly synched up. Do you feel like ladder climbing?"

"Can they slow down the rotation?" asked Bean.

"We can ask, but . . . they chose this rate of rotation for a reason. It's right for the plants."

"And you don't think they'll risk the plants."

"The biota is part of their mission. We not only aren't bringing them the cocooned Hive Queen they believe that humans have, we also want to jeopardize the gravity the plants require?"

Ender interrupted. "They're probably already reading the images in our minds."

"I don't have any images," said Carlotta.

"Yes you do," said Ender.

"Is that so?" said Bean. "All right, do this. Think of

yourselves standing next to me. The size you are, the size I am. Me lying here in the cargo bay, you standing beside me. Picture that."

"Eh, we pictured it as you said it," said Carlotta. "We had no choice."

"What did that accomplish?" asked Cincinnatus.

"Think about it," said Bean.

They did. Cincinnatus got it first. "Toguro," he said. "You're about the same size relative to us that the Hive Queen was relative to them."

"Close enough," said Bean.

"And you're our father," said Ender, "the way the Hive Queen was their mother."

"But not our *mate*," said Carlotta. "No way are you a Hive Queen."

"Don't even pretend that I am," said Bean. "Just let them see the sizes, say that I'm your only living parent, and the only way I can come to you in the ark is if they slow down the rotation of the ecotat. Tell them how much. Let them figure out what will happen to the soil and the roots."

"They'll ask how long they need to slow the rotation," said Ender. "Because it will affect plant growth patterns."

"Then tell them it needs to stay slow until I die or I return to this ship. Tell them that I'm not likely to live very long, but I want to meet them in their ark before I die. If I'm still alive after I've talked to them enough, then I'll come back here, and they can spin up to normal."

"How long is 'enough'?" asked Ender.

"I hate this whole idea," murmured Carlotta.

"Until I understand as much as I can about what happened to their Hive Queen. Tell them I need to know why she died, so that I can be sure you won't get poisoned when you transfer to the Ark."

Consternation from the three of them.

"I told you already," said Bean. "The planet down there is your future. You need to move the entire lab into the ecotat and set about creating gut bacteria that will digest the alien proteins and make them useful for yourselves and your children to come. When you can live entirely within the Formic ecotat and what it produces, then you're ready to colonize that planet."

"What if we don't want to?" That was Cincinnatus.

"You want to," said Bean. "Because you want our species to survive, and there's no better chance, anywhere. We've had this conversation. Only now we're having it where the drones can see the images that pass through your minds."

"Why do you think the drones will go along with this?" asked Ender. "Their own species is dying out—they're the last, with no hope of reproduction."

"Tell them that I am your father. A male. And when I die, they must adopt you and become your fathers. Teach you everything they know. Tell them that we're not really human—we're different from the rest of that species. So that when you populate that planet, you do it as a new sentient species, and you will always regard these drones as your fathers."

"I don't think they have a concept of adoption," said Ender.

"Of course they do. Remember? You said that when the Hive Queen died without eating them first, they felt honored, because it meant they were being passed to the new Hive Queen. Except they couldn't find one."

"That's not adoption, it's remarriage," said Cincinnatus.

"Close enough," said Bean. "Tell them. Try to make them see analogies between their species, their *lives,* and ours. Let them understand how small you are and how short a life you'll have. You need all the help you can get to survive."

"Why not?" said Carlotta. "We're not even lying."

"You never knew the Hive Queen, but through them, you can become *like* children of the Hive Queen," said Bean.

"We've got it, Father," said Ender. "You don't have to give us a script."

So the children negotiated. This time drones touched all three of them, and afterward they said it was astonishing, because they could sense each other through the drones. It allowed them to join their images together, unify them. The plan was worked out, agreed to by drones and children.

Then the children came back. Bean piloted the Hound for them again, and this time docked it directly over the cargo bay. The *Herodotus* was designed for this, and soon the doors opened and a much higher ceiling loomed above Bean.

He had not realized how claustrophobic he had felt all these years, how the ceiling had oppressed him as he grew larger and larger. But when it was removed, he felt a great lightening of his spirit. He was almost cheerful.

The children weren't. They were afraid that they would accidently kill him somehow in the transfer. "That's not fair," said Carlotta. "To put that guilt on us."

"No guilt," said Bean. "I'd rather die doing something than lying here like a melon."

They had never seen a melon growing on the ground.

There was work to do before the transfer. Bean insisted that they transfer all the lab equipment first. He also showed all three of them the secret cargo compartments and demonstrated the use of the artificial wombs—without, of course, inserting anything into them. "In vitro fertilization is a common practice, as is egg extraction," said Bean. "You can learn about it over the ansible. The wombs aren't so common because they're illegal on a lot of worlds."

"Why?" asked Carlotta.

"Because they're unnatural," said Bean. "Or they deprive surrogate mothers of a livelihood. Lots of reasons, but it comes down to the real reason: Artificial wombs suggest that women aren't necessary, and that really bothers a lot of women."

"But women still produce the ova," said Carlotta.

"There are ways around that," said Bean. "And ways around men, too. Neither sex actually needs the other in order to reproduce. But several societies have tried doing without it, and evolution ends up winning—the discontent grows and the society either goes back to mating or people keep leaving until only a tiny fanatical remnant remain. It's the human race, Carlotta. Why should it make sense?"

So Bean watched and tried not to fret as the children learned from the drones how to build sealed laboratories in the ecotat. It was a technology well known on the ark, because when they reached the planet's surface it would take time to find or dig tunnels and caves. They had to use the plan for a temporary Hive Queen's chamber, because no other space was tall enough for the adult-size equipment to fit.

As soon as the lab was up and working, Ender simply withdrew from any further preparation for Bean's move. "I think there might be something in the Formic genome that will help us. And not just to digest food."

So it was Cincinnatus and Carlotta who made all the preparations. There was some serious discussion of trying to fashion a pressure suit for Bean. "In case some seal is broken and we lose atmosphere," she said.

Bean laughed. "Carlotta, my darling girl, you're so compassionate. But if a seal is broken, I'll die. If you go into space, you put your faith in machinery, and hope it works."

"But what if—"

"Carlotta, the pressure suit would kill me even if you could make it work. It creates *pressure,* but it's not the same as a normal atmosphere. It can't be. So I'd die anyway, and then you'd have the problem of getting me out of the suit so my body materials could be added to the ecotat."

Carlotta burst into tears.

"Father," said Cincinnatus, "you're so sensitive to your daughter's tender feelings."

"Did she imagine I'd be buried? Cremated? Ejected into

space? You told her yourself, back when you were planning to dispose of me—my body hoards too many resources."

"That was before we met up with the ark," said Cincinnatus. "And I'm not proud of the boy I was then."

"You're still the same boy," said Bean. "Always thinking six steps ahead. And impatient. I don't hold it against you, but I don't forget it, especially the bits where you were right."

"Weren't many of those."

"By and large, all three of you kids run above the human average on being right, and you learn from your mistakes."

"The Giant says that I'm an idiot, but I'm an above average idiot."

"That's about right," said Bean.

Bean had imagined that he might make the transfer in just a few days, but Carlotta was methodical and slow, testing everything. She also insisted on moving a lot of computers out of *Herodotus* and getting them powered up and networked in the ecotat. And then the big one.

"I want to move the ansible," she said.

Bean hadn't anticipated that one. "Eventually," he said. "But your network is reaching between the ships just fine. You can access human communications systems just fine from there."

"I'm going to build another," she said. "For redundancy. I need it there so I don't have to keep going back and forth to work on it."

"The ansible technology is still a closely guarded secret," said Bean.

"Ender and I hacked the tech years ago," said Carlotta. "We thought you'd be angry so we didn't tell you."

"You hacked the parts of the technology that they made hackable," said Bean. "I watched you do it."

"We found the rest of it later, and hacked that, too. While you slept. Give me some credit." ·

So it took longer than Bean thought, and he hated it when the ansible was in transit, fearing damage to that machine more than he feared damage to himself. The ansible was their lifeline to the human race. It was Bean's lifeline to his last living friend—Ender Wiggin. Not that they ever talked or even sent messages. For all Bean knew, Ender Wiggin never thought of Bean at all, or if he did, he assumed Bean had died years ago. Wiggin was hiding from everybody, from Ender the Xenocide. He was a speaker for the dead now. Nobody knew he was *the* Speaker for the Dead. They just took him to be another of the growing number of itinerant speakers. It was a good calling for him. But it made Ender Wiggin focus on living people and the recently dead whom they summoned him to speak for. He had no time for his past. Indeed, he was running from his past, in all likelihood. Bean imagined it would not be a friendly act to make himself known to Ender Wiggin now. Ender would wonder what he wanted. Ender would wish he hadn't contacted him.

But if the Hive Queen had lied to Ender, if *The Hive Queen* was based on lies, then Ender was devoting his life to protecting a fraud, looking for a home for a Hive Queen who had her own agenda and wasn't telling Ender what it was.

If that turned out to be true, Bean would find a way to get the message to Ender, even if he didn't let him know the true identity of the sender.

At last it was time for Bean to make the voyage.

It had been hard enough for him to walk into *Herodotus* when he took the toddlers aboard and left Petra and the other babies—for their normal children truly were still babies then, just learning to talk, toddling about on unsteady legs. He hadn't cared much about the uselessness of the enlargements that had been attempted. He knew that even the taller table and larger chair would soon be useless to him. He wasn't going to make another. He knew from the start that he would end up lying on his back or his side in the cargo bay, with gravity set as close to nothing as possible.

But he *had* walked onto the ship. Now Carlotta cut the gravity to nothing, then turned on the gravitator she had rigged on the Hound. It drew him upward very slowly. She and Cincinnatus rose with him, rotating him slowly in midair, so that when he reached the padded flooring of the Hound, he settled into it very gently.

He had been terrified the entire time. Weightlessness had once felt almost normal to him, but at his size, the sense of falling that came with weightlessness—cresting the peak of a rollercoaster, only it kept on and on—was not a thrill, it felt like death. He would never survive a real fall. Even tripping and falling headlong would shatter brittle bones and he would never recover. Human bodies weren't designed to be four and a half meters tall.

Carlotta's design and her and Cincinnatus's execution of it were perfect. Except for the fear, Bean suffered no damage at all. Not even bruising, not even sore muscles, so gentle was his coming to rest on the floor of the Hound.

Only when he was in place did he realize that there was no computer beside him. "Carlotta," he said, "we can't go until I'm rigged to control the Hound. Bring me my holotop."

She laughed. "We know how you pilot ships, Father. You're deft at it, but the trajectory you used on every trip you've piloted for us would kill you. Cincinnatus is taking you, and instead of an hour, the trip is going to take the best part of a day. So snuggle in and sleep."

"With Cincinnatus steering the ship?"

But Bean allowed himself to feel relieved instead of annoyed. He had been piloting the Hound from a stable position in the cargo hold of the *Herodotus*. When he was inside the Hound, his position would not be stable—he would be experiencing all the inertia changes of the flight, without being in the pilot's seat. The children had anticipated a problem and found a good solution.

Not a perfect one—Cincinnatus's inexperience showed now and then. But it was a better flight than Bean would have given himself, and as they drifted into the open airlock in the side of the ark, Bean could only admire how deftly Cincinnatus brought the Hound to a stop in the middle of the air.

There was no gravitator here—gravity lensing did not work

well inside rotating objects, especially this near a planet. You either had gravity lensing *or* centrifugal force, not both.

The bay in the wheel was long enough that Bean's body didn't stick out of the inner side. Good design, he thought. Highly recommended for giants.

The real ingenuity—and the reason it had taken a week—became visible as soon as the wheel synched with the very slow ecotat cylinder. This high off the ground, Bean felt almost no gravity. Then the door opened and he saw the ecotat with his own eyes for the first time.

The relief he had felt when the ceiling lifted in the *Herodotus* had been nothing compared to this. It was so large, and the false sun in the center of the opposite hub gave such a sincere imitation of sunlight that Bean felt for a dizzying moment as if he had come back home to Earth.

Then he saw how the world bent upward in both directions, and formed a clearly visible ceiling overhead, with trees and meadows and even small lakes—ponds, really. But there were birds flying—had anyone mentioned the birds?—and while the trees were all from the Formic worlds, Bean had never become an expert on the trees of Earth. They were forest enough for him. The green took his breath away; the strange colors here and there still seemed to belong.

It wasn't a planet, but it was as close to one as he would ever come. He had never thought to be in a living world like this again.

Carlotta and Cincinnatus had rigged a scaffolding opposite

the door, and as they drew him from the bay in the wheel, Bean realized that the cloth under him was a sturdy cargo net—a hammock, but with rods to keep it from collapsing into a wad with him folded up inside it.

When he was completely free of the door, he was resting comfortably within the hammock. Then they swayed him down like good sailors, and the illusion of gravity grew for him as gently and naturally as if he had climbed down a ladder.

It was just a bit more gravity than he had been used to. He had to breathe just a little more deeply and often. But he wasn't panting. He could do this. He could live this way. For a while.

When he was at rest on the ground, the cloth of the hammock under him, the birds came swooping down, and he realized they were not birds at all. They were the drones.

They hovered around him, then came to rest on the ground. Ender came then—the lab wasn't far away—and he seemed happy. Too happy for the occasion, really—his lab work must be going well. Bean had been tracking his lines of research as best he could—but Carlotta had set up this network, and Bean found that she had blocked, or simply not created, the back doors and surreptitious channels he had used constantly on the *Herodotus*. They were cutting him loose from his close supervision of their lives, even as they solemnly obeyed him in all his overt decisions.

"They want to begin at once," said Ender. "Talking to you."

"Before you die," said Cincinnatus dryly.

"Then we'll start at once," said Bean.

The drones flew up to his chest. They seemed to weigh almost nothing. Then Bean realized they were still bearing much of their weight with their wings.

"They can't be on my chest," said Bean. "Small though they are, I can't bear the weight and still breathe. But if they stand on the ground beside me, they can touch my head the way they touched yours."

"They want to honor you as their new Hive Queen," said Ender, "but they don't wish to kill you in the process." Ender knelt and touched his head to the mouth of one of the drones. In a moment the message was conveyed. The drones slipped off Bean's body and gathered around his head.

The drones had become more skilled at communicating with a human than when they had first tried to speak with Ender. The images came slowly, gently, and feelings were not pushed hard. Suggestions, really.

At first Bean spoke aloud what he was getting from the drones. Ender, who was also touching them and seeing all, affirmed for him that he was understanding them well.

Soon it was Carlotta who kept him company. And then Cincinnatus took his turn. The drones also worked in shifts, two at a time staying with him.

For they kept at it day and night, waking and sleeping. In truth, it felt to Bean as though he were mostly asleep the entire time. It was a long, sweet, fascinating dream, the whole story of the lives of the drones, everything they knew about their Hive Queen, the other queens, the lives of the workers, the history of everything. They knew so much—and knew it directly, without the distractions of language.

But as the dream went on, hour after hour, day after day, Bean could see the holes that had been left in their knowledge. He would ask, and they gave the answer they thought he wanted; they could not see what they could not see. They thought they knew everything, but Bean could see how the Hive Queen had shut them out from the most vital, dangerous information.

Bean had believed, like the rest of the human race, that an entire colony of Formics had only a single mind. That the workers were to the Hive Queen as fingers and feet were to humans—just a part of her, with no minds of their own. But as Bean tasted their small lives in the memory of the drones, he knew that this was a lie, a deep and terrible lie. The workers had minds, had thoughts, had desires, but these were only used as the Hive Queen wanted to use them, and were swept aside as irrelevant when she had no use. If a worker resisted her will, even to suggest a better course, she would simply leave the worker's mind, close the link between them, and through the eyes of nearby Formics she would watch the resistant worker die.

And she was satisfied with that. Because the deepest fear of the Hive Queens was a rebellion of the workers. The drones had no memory of such a thing—how could they?—but Bean knew that the Hive Queen's relief spoke of tension she hadn't let the drones experience. She hid her fear from them, as she hid it from all. But Bean had the mind-reading skill of a human. Unable to connect directly, humans had to become adept at reading emotions from outward signs. Most humans did it only just well enough; some did it very badly. Bean had become superb at it, but not from love. Love makes you a bad observer—you put the best interpretation on everything. Hate is as blinding—you assume the worst. For sheer survival as a child, Bean had become adroit at discerning the likely actions of people from the outward cues they showed without meaning to. The Hive Queen had no such recognizable signs—no facial expressions that Bean could read. He didn't have to— she hid the feelings she knew she should hide, but not the subsequent ones, and Bean could guess what the Hive Queen had felt just before. He was confident that his interpretations were consistently good, or if not, they were certainly as good as he was going to get.

Three days he lived in the dream. Unlike the Hive Queens, Bean did not attempt to hide anything. His whole life he laid bare before the drones. Let them feel what it meant to be a human, a man—one with responsibilities to others, but ultimately an agent unto himself, free to choose as long as he also accepted the consequences of his choices.

They marveled. They were horrified at some things—at the idea of murder. Bean let them see that he thought it was murder when the Hive Queen broke off contact with the mind of a worker, killing her. But the drones were merely amused at his obvious misinterpretation. Not like you, she's not like you humans, you don't understand. They didn't say those words, but he understood the idea from their amused, patient, dismissive feelings. Like adults talking to precocious children. Like Bean talking to his own children when they weren't yet two and had not yet begun to educate themselves completely on their own.

At last the drones withdrew themselves, and then Bean slept for real, deeply, completely. Not dreamlessly, but they were the comfortable dreams of ordinary sleep. No nightmares.

And then he awoke and it was broad daylight. An awning kept direct sunlight off his face. It was warm and the air was a little damp. "We covered you while it rained last night," said Carlotta. "They have to make it rain at least once every four days when they're doing summer, as they are right now. They held off during your conversation."

"What was the outcome of it?" asked Bean.

"Isn't that for you to say?" asked Carlotta.

"I learned much, but what was most interesting were the things the Hive Queen never showed them. They didn't believe that anything was left out, they believed she was completely open to them, but what else could they believe? Their lives were surrounded by the lies she wove for them."

"Parents do that to protect their children, I heard," said Carlotta.

"I heard that too," said Bean. "And it's probably necessary. Just frustrating for an inquirer like me."

"How are you feeling?" she asked him.

"Physically? Look at the machinery and tell me whether I'm alive or not."

"Good heartbeat," she said. "Other vitals fine—for a man your size."

"I don't think I've eaten," said Bean. "But the other equipment is in place. Have I been processing bodily wastes efficiently?"

"Poo and pee are all up to snuff. The local worms turned up their noses at it, but the plants are happy, or at least none of them have died yet."

"Then my life has meaning."

He slept again. When next he woke, it was dusk, and all three children were gathered around him.

"Father," said Ender. "I have something to tell you. Good and bad. Good, mostly."

"Then tell me," said Bean. "I don't want to die during a preamble. Get to the meat."

"Then here it is," said Ender. "The Formics have inadvertently taught me how to cure our condition. We can turn on the normal human patterns of growth and then the end of growth, without switching off Anton's Key."

"How?" asked Bean.

"When we saw how the Formic workers died when they were cut off from the Queen, I began to think, they don't love her, it's not as if their heart is broken. In fact, they should experience her death as a liberation, and yet they die. So I suspected that the queens had changed the workers' genome somehow, the way they changed the rabs. But I was wrong. The genome of the Formics in the dried-up cocoons was essentially identical to those of the drones and of the Hive Queen herself. It's not in the genome, these differences."

"What then?" asked Bean. "Don't make me guess."

"They do it with organelles. Like our mitochondria. The queens could mix up a bacterial soup in glands that are only vestigial in the workers and drones. Then they infect the eggs of workers with these bacteria, and the bacteria take up residence in every cell in their bodies.

"The organelles are responsive to the mental connection between the Queen and the workers. They sense whether it's there. And if it isn't, they shut down the metabolism of every cell in the body, virtually at once."

"Organelles as thought police," said Carlotta bitterly. "Bitches."

"Tyrants," said Bean. "They used to have to worry all the time about revolts among their daughters. The organelle gave them peace of mind. Allowed them to have far more daughters than they could dominate directly with their minds."

"Yes," said Ender. "The drones are the natural adaptation. They are able to extend the Queen's reach. But even with twenty males attached to her, she could only control at most a few hundred workers at a time. Some were bound to slip out of her control. So a queen invented the enslaving organelle. Or maybe lots of queens tried different ones and shared the results until they settled on this one."

"And they never gave it to the males," said Bean.

"They didn't need it. They were permanently on the Queen's team, no matter what. Adoring, attached to her, constantly aware of every thought she had—"

"Every thought she wanted them to be aware of," corrected Bean.

Ender nodded. "Every queen mixes up this organelle inside herself and administers it to the worker eggs. The males are natural—they are what evolution made them. But the queens do this to the workers one by one. They are all aware of exactly what they're doing."

"Creating the ultimate serfs," said Cincinnatus. "And the perfect soldiers. They fight and die when she tells them to. If they balk, she'll cut them off and they die anyway. It's a desperate kind of life for them. Maybe when she's actually concentrating on them they love her as the males do. But then her attention moves somewhere else. The connection is still there—has to be, or they die—and they still don't dare to even experience their own hate. But it's there, don't you think?"

"More in some than in others," said Bean. "The terrible secret of the Hive Queens. But Ender, how did this help you in any way with the problem of the antonines?"

"Leguminotes," said Cincinnatus.

Bean liked hearing them insist on using that form of his name.

"Organelles. We were trying to work directly on the genome of living individuals. Volescu created our variation when we were embryos, just a handful of cells. But living organisms with millions of cells? Changing the genome on the fly has been tried again and again, with some good effect when the changes were very simple."

Bean knew the history. "The giantism is inseparable from the intelligence, so it can't be done."

"But the giantism isn't an effect—it's the *absence* of an off switch, or rather a patterning switch. We can't add that off switch in the genome without wrecking the intelligence. But we can put the off switch in an organelle."

Just that simple. Obvious now that Ender said it. But not obvious, after all. "You can't just make organelles for humans," said Bean. "We've had mitochondria for so long that—they joined the cells long before there were humans. The mitochondria reproduce when the cells divide. The Hive Queens had to insert their organelles into every egg."

"Right," said Ender.

"This is the clever part," said Carlotta.

"We use a virus to insert the snippet of altered gene into the naturally occurring mitochondria. They get the off switch and then express it at the appropriate time."

"We think," said Cincinnatus.

"Well, it's not as if we've reached puberty yet," said Ender. "We have to wait and see. But one thing is certain—the change has gone through every cell in our bodies."

"You've already done it?" said Bean. His heart raced.

"Calm, calm, Father," said Carlotta.

"Of course we did it," said Cincinnatus. "What possible reason would we have for waiting?"

"My permission?" said Bean.

"We had that already," said Cincinnatus. "When you told us your plan for this world. It's ours. These bodies are ours. You would have told us to consider very carefully and you would have weighed the pros and cons for us and then you would have let us decide. So we did those things just as if you had been awake, and we decided, and Ender blew an aerosol of the virus into our lungs and we got just a little sick as it went through our bodies."

"And now we're better, and our bodies aren't rejecting the change," said Carlotta.

"And in a few years, we'll see if it worked," said Ender. "If not, we'll still have time to try again. Or try something else. But no matter what, this change will be passed on automatically to our children. The leguminotes won't have to take some kind of pill or get some alteration in order to have normal growth triggered by genes inside our mitochondria. We'll pass it on to our children."

"Technically speaking," said Carlotta, "I'll pass it on."

"No argument there," said Ender.

Bean could feel the tears dripping out of the corners of his eyes. It wasn't worth the effort to try to move his arms to brush them away. Let them water the soil of this place.

"So . . . pretty good work, neh?" said Ender.

"Oh, very good," said Bean.

"The question is," began Cincinnatus.

"No," said Bean.

"You don't even want to hear the question?" asked Carlotta.

"You want to give this treatment to me now. But it's too late. What made you a little sick would probably kill me. And suppose it worked? I'm already so large that my heart can't keep me alive if I do anything more than lie here and vegetate."

"You think all the time," said Carlotta. "You're still getting enough blood to your brain."

"But I don't *need* to think all the time anymore," said Bean. "You did this yourselves. You handled an expedition into an alien vessel. You saved a dying group of aliens, as far as they could be saved. You're going to adapt yourselves to eat alien proteins—"

"We're going to introduce some Earthborn plants and animals, too," said Cincinnatus. "Carlotta can't live without potatoes."

"And you cured your own fatal genetic illness," said Bean. "All you need to do now is keep your existence a complete secret from the ordinary human race."

"We know," said Carlotta. "That's why we took the ansible away from you."

The words hung there in the silence.

"You were going to tell your friend Ender Wiggin the truth about the Hive Queens, weren't you?" she said.

"Yes," said Bean.

"We knew you would," said Cincinnatus. "But Wiggin doesn't know how to keep his mouth shut. He wrote *The Hive Queen*. He tells the *truth* even when the results are terrible."

"We have to stay hidden," said Ender. "And keep the existence of this ark a secret, too, because if the International Fleet knows about this one, they're bound to guess that there are other colony ships, ones where the Queen didn't die, and then they'll go looking for them."

"We promised the drones that we wouldn't let you put the

survival of the Formic species at risk that way," said Cincin-natus. "That was the reason they agreed to cooperate."

So he wouldn't be sending a message to Ender Wiggin after all. And that was better. Ender didn't need to hear from him, not at this late date. And what good would the warning do? If he knew Ender Wiggin—and he knew him better than anyone, except perhaps his sister, Valentine—he'd go ahead and restore the cocooned Queen when he found a suitable place, regardless of any warning.

"Even that was done well," said Bean. "You uppity little bastards."

"We come from married parents," corrected Carlotta. "Or so you told us."

He slept well that night, better than he had in five long years in space, because his children were safe, and perhaps cured, and certainly able to take care of themselves. He had accomplished it all—if not directly, then by raising them to be the kind of people who would dare to take the steps nec-essary to save themselves.

In the morning, they were all busy, but Bean was content to lie there and listen to the sounds of life in the meadow. He didn't know the names of any of the animals, but there were some who hopped and some that chirped and croaked, and some that landed lightly on him and crawled or wriggled to somewhere else and dropped or leapt off of him. He was part of the life here. Soon his body would be even more deeply involved with it. Meanwhile, he was happy.

And maybe when he died, he'd find out that one religion

or another was right after all. Maybe Petra would be there waiting for him—impatient, scolding. "What took you?"

"I had to finish my work."

"Well, you didn't—the children had to do it."

And others. Sister Carlotta, who saved his life. Poke, who also saved his life, and died for it. His parents, though he didn't meet them until after the war. His brother Nikolai.

Bean woke again. He hadn't known he was going to fall asleep. But now the children were gathered around him, looking serious.

"You had a little heart incident," said Cincinnatus.

"It's called happiness," said Bean.

"A new name," said Carlotta. "I'm not sure it'll catch on."

"But it's beating now," said Bean.

"Too fast, but yes," said Cincinnatus.

"I want to tell you something," said Bean. "Your mother was the love of my life."

"We know," said Carlotta.

"I loved other people, but her most, her best. Because we made something together. We made you."

Bean began to roll on his side.

"Whoa! What are you doing?" demanded Cincinnatus.

"I'm not accountable to you," said Bean. "I'm the parent. I'm the *Giant.*"

"You just had an episode," said Ender.

"You think I can't feel the difference in my own chest?" said Bean.

He propped himself carefully on his elbows and knees. A

position he had not adopted in at least a year, ever since he stopped trying to roll over. He hadn't been sure he could even do it. But there he was, on elbows and knees, like a baby. Panting, exhausted. I can't do this.

"What I want," he said softly, "is to stand in this meadow and walk in the light of the sun."

"Why didn't you say so?" said Carlotta.

They got him to lie back down on the hammock cloth, and then they winched him up to sitting position, and then stood him up on his feet.

The gravity he felt was so slight, so very close to nothing, yet being upright, even with the hammock holding him a little, was taking all his breath.

"I'm going to walk now," he said.

His legs were rubbery under him.

The drones flew to him and clung to his clothing, fluttering to help hold him up. The children gathered around his legs and helped him take one step, then another.

He felt the sun on his face. He felt the ground under his feet. He felt the people who loved him holding on to him and bearing him along.

It was enough.

"I'm going to lie down now," said Bean.

And then he did.

And then he died.